SAY YOU'RE MINE

a Shillings Agency novel

DIANE ALBERTS

Entangled Publishing, LLC
2614 South Timberline Road
Suite 109
Fort Collins, CO 80525
Visit our website at www.entangledpublishing.com.

Brazen is an imprint of Entangled Publishing, LLC. For more information on our titles, visit www.brazenbooks.com.

Edited by Candace Havens
Cover design by Heather Howland
Cover art from Deposit Photos

Manufactured in the United States of America

First Edition December 2015

ENTANGLED
BRAZEN

This one's for Joanne. You do what you want, when you want, and you rock it.

Chapter One

Steven Thomas lived in the ninth level of hell, or so he'd been told enough times. Mostly by women who hated him, because he slept with them and didn't call them back. He was always up-front about his expectations of women, and never led them to believe he was looking for more than a one-night stand, yet they never seemed to believe him. Even with all that, he was pretty damn certain they were right.

As if being a Navy SEAL doing morally questionable things in the name of freedom and country wasn't enough to fuck him over with the big man upstairs, the way he'd been acting ever since he returned to civilization *would* be. Maybe there was no saving him, but after getting shot overseas and almost dying, he was determined to have the best time possible before jumping into that fiery pit with a grin on his face.

But he wasn't fighting overseas anymore. Now, he was a security agent at the Shillings Agency, and he protected rich dudes while they golfed.

Another thing he was trying to accept.

Till he figured out what came next, he was going to have fun. Live life. Drink merrily. Screw beautiful women. Be wild and free. After all the shit he'd done, he was never, *ever* settling down. It wasn't in his blood—unlike his best friend, Holt Cunningham, who had settled down with Steven's baby sister.

The little fucker…

"Dude." Holt sat next to him, letting out a long breath as he settled in. "Why do you look like you're about to go all Dalek on a bunch of Cybermen?"

Steven rolled his eyes at Holt's *Doctor Who* reference, and downed the last of his drink. It burned going down—just the way he liked it. It blurred his vision a little bit more—also the way he liked it. "If I was going to delete anyone from this universe, it would be you, dumbass."

"Ah." Holt sighed and leaned on the bar, completely unfazed by the threat to his safety. His brown hair was messed up to perfection—as it always was—and he studied Steven with somber blue eyes. "What did I do this time?"

"Besides falling for my sister…?"

"Guilty as charged. And I'd do it all over again." Holt grinned, staring across the bar at something. That "something" was more than likely Steven's sister, Lydia. "But that's not what's bugging you. It's been a year."

A year. A whole damn year.

"She's not drinking tonight," Steven said, having his suspicions as to *why* she wasn't.

"Yeah." Holt flushed and ruffled his hair. Steven's instincts were spot on. That was Holt's tic, when he was trying to hide something. Steven was good at reading people, and even better at spotting evasion. "And? Why is that so weird? She likes soda, too."

He could call him on it. Ask Holt point-blank if he'd gotten his sister pregnant. Despite his avoidance, his friend wasn't typically a liar. But if they weren't ready to tell anyone yet, he could wait patiently. He wouldn't be upset about a baby, so the couple's secrecy was odd. The idea of a little niece or nephew felt...*nice.*

"Is she feeling okay?" Steven asked. He needed to find out that much, at least. "Like, is she all right?"

"Yeah. She just had an upset stomach earlier," Holt muttered, still not looking at him. "She'll be fine."

In nine months. "Good."

"We're going to be expected to dance soon. Did you bring Lauren?"

Without really wanting to, Steven scanned the room for the familiar brunette. Lauren Brixton. His *other* best friend. She stood off to the side, chatting up some tall, blond man he vaguely recognized from accounting.

Why the hell was she talking to that dude?

He was a prick, and everyone knew it.

"Yeah." Steven shifted his weight on the stool, narrowing his eyes when she placed her hand on the asshole's arm. "She came as my plus one."

"These work events are too boring without one." Holt flagged down the bartender, his glasses askew and his black suit jacket unbuttoned. "I'll take another Coke, please. And a ginger ale, too."

So. Holt wasn't drinking because Lydia wasn't.

He liked that.

Lifting his hand, he held his empty glass up. "And I'll have another whiskey."

Holt frowned. "What is that? Your fourth?"

"Yeah, maybe?"

"We've only been here an hour, man." Holt adjusted his glasses. "Slow down, or I'll have to carry your drunk ass out of here...again."

"The way I see it, you owe me at least ten more of those

nights," Steven said, keeping his voice light even though Holt was pissing him off. After all, Holt had no room to talk. A year ago, he'd been drinking heavily and spending all his free time in bars, and Steven had been the one telling *him* to slow down.

So what the hell ever.

Lauren watched him from across the room, so he waved. She smiled and returned the gesture, but turned back to the prick occupying her time. Anger rolled through his veins when the asshole leaned in closer to speak into her ear, and she flushed in reply, but he ignored the unwanted emotion. It was just Lauren, not some girl he was trying to fuck.

If she liked flirting with the jerk-off, then so be it.

He turned back to Holt, who watched him with a smirk. "What now?"

"Nothing." Holt rubbed his jaw and shook his head. "Nothing at all. Hey, how's Lauren doing with that Brian guy?"

Brian. Shit, he hated that guy. He was using Lauren, and the sooner she saw it, the better. Plus, when he laughed, he sounded like a damn otter. Kind of acted like one, too. "Ask her yourself. I don't give a damn how he is, or how she feels about him. He's just another guy she'll date, then realize isn't good enough for her, and I'll be the one comforting her after he's gone—until she finds another asshole to try and fix."

"Easy man." Holt shoved his glasses into place with his pointer finger. "Your jealousy's showing."

The hell it was. He and Lauren had been friends for over twenty years—and that was it. *Friends.* They'd never crossed the line, or even discussed crossing the line. She'd never once acted as if she ever thought about more. He would've noticed.

But everyone else was convinced they were soul mates.

They *weren't*.

Just because he had yet to like a man she'd brought home didn't mean he was jealous, or that he secretly loved her. It meant that she had horrible taste in men.

That was fact, not opinion.

"Whatever you say, man," Steven said, dragging a hand through his hair. A classical song started in the background, and people milled to the dance floor—including their boss, Cooper Shillings. He scowled at them and cocked his head toward the dance floor. Shit. He hated dancing. Give him a gun and a desert over a tux and a ballroom, anytime. "Cooper's giving us the look."

Holt sighed, grabbed his soda, and tugged on his bow tie. "Guess it's time to dance, huh?"

"Guess so." He picked up his whiskey and held it out to his buddy, grinning. "But first? I'll finish this. To leave it here unfinished would be alcohol abuse."

His best friend stared back at him, looking 100 percent *not* amused. "You forget I've done this already." Then he leaned in, nostrils flaring. "Drinking to drown the pain doesn't work. Nothing does."

"It worked pretty damn well for you, didn't it?" He tipped his head to his sister—a former one-night stand of Holt's. "You found her in a bar, while drinking."

"Yeah." The other man watched Lydia with devotion and love as she made her way across the room to him. "But that was pure luck."

"Well, we can't all be so lucky, can we?"

He might be drinking and fucking too much, but it was the only thing that dulled the screams that haunted him daily. The only thing that dulled the guilt that he'd lived, when the rest of his platoon hadn't, and it eased the anger over that fact—fuck, the *anger*. Every time he remembered what happened over there, he wanted to shoot someone.

So he took a different kind of shot instead.

If he'd known what they truly were walking into, if he'd had even a damn inkling of the type of danger they'd faced, his men would be alive today. If his superior officer hadn't led him to believe he was bringing his men on a routine mission that held no danger, when in fact it was an ambush, his men would still be here, and he wouldn't have gotten shot—and put out of the game permanently.

He fucking *hated* liars.

Every single one.

He glanced over his shoulder. Lauren walked beside Lydia. Something about the way she moved tonight made it impossible to look away. Damn it, she was intoxicating, with her hips swaying seductively as she made her way across the room to him. Her dark hair fell over her shoulders and tits, and she was easily the prettiest woman here.

She was his one constant, in a world full of chaos.

And she would never lie to him.

He tossed back the rest of his whiskey, shaking his head at the burn. "Damn. That felt pretty damn good."

Holt shifted beside him. "Steven—"

"Dude, I'm fine. I'm just thirsty, is all." Steven set the empty glass down. That last shot blurred his vision even more, drowning out the memories. The nightmares. The loss. "Now cheer up. It's time to go dance with our women."

He smiled at Lauren, and she grinned back. The prick she'd been chatting with stood by the wall, alone, looking all sad-faced panda bear. That shouldn't have pleased him so much…but it did. It didn't mean he was jealous, though.

He'd die for her. Kill for her. Fight for her. But not *love* her. He didn't do love. Didn't want it. Hell, he didn't deserve it. Guys like him didn't get to be loved.

"Hey. It's my two favorite men," Lydia said, hugging Steven tight. "You two doing good?"

"Of course we are," Holt said.

Steven hugged her and squeezed tight, breathing her scent in. She was the only woman who held his heart. His baby sister. And, damn it all to hell, she was all grown up now. She needed to knock that shit off. Her secret almost made him throw her over his shoulder and run for the door so he could keep her safe forever and ever, just like he had when they were kids. That was Holt's job now, though. "How are you, Lyd?"

"Great." She beamed at Holt and moved out of his arms. It was a hell of a lot harder to let go of her than it should have been. As soon as he did, she went over to Holt, sliding into his arms naturally. "You're looking quite handsome in your navy blue suit. And bow tie."

"Bow ties are cool," Holt said, quoting *Doctor Who*.

Lydia and Steven laughed.

Lauren looked lost. She didn't watch *Doctor Who* like the rest of them.

It was her only fault.

He winked at her. "Lauren picked it out to match her dress, after calling me color-blind."

"He planned on wearing black," she said, exasperation in her tone. "The man might be able to charge into an armored building full of insurgents without a weapon, and come out alive, but he can't match colors to save his *life*."

She rested her hand on his shoulder, like she had a million times before.

This time, though, her touch burned through his suit jacket, and it unsettled him in ways it never had before, which didn't make sense. But, *damn*, she looked good tonight. And he needed to cut back on the drinking. The desire he felt for her was unexplainable. It had to be the booze fucking with his head.

He turned to her, laughing despite the unwanted desire rushing south at the speed of light. "It's not my fault. Navy blue and black have always, and will always, look the same to me. I look at you and I see…black. Nothing but black."

"Look again," she said, raising a brow.

Always one to follow her wishes, he glanced up and down her trim length. It was as flawless as always. Generously sized, perky tits—which he knew for a fact were 32D, because he'd gone to the mall with her once, and she'd made him go into Victoria's Secret with her, which had been pure *hell*—thin waist, generously curved hips that never failed to draw his eye, and a fine ass that had driven many men crazy.

But not him. Never him.

And if he said it enough times…maybe he'd believe it.

He'd always admired her. Her smart brain. Her sharp wit. The way she laughed, all full and rich, and how much she cared for everyone around her. And when she smiled at something sweet, it stole the air straight outta people's chests—particularly his.

And there was her body, which was, hands down, one of the finest damn bodies he had ever seen. He might only be her friend, but he wasn't blind *or* stupid. She was the most beautiful woman he'd ever met. The real kick in the ass was she was just as gorgeous inside as she was out.

But tonight, the outside was a hell of a lot prettier.

She stood there, smiling at him, asking him to *look* at her, and it did things to him. Things that had nothing to do with friendship, and everything to do with getting her out of that tight black dress ASAP, and into his arms. "Trust me, cupcake. I'm looking."

"Yeah." Her cheeks flushed pink, and she cleared her throat. "I see that."

"Well. This just got really awkward, really fast." Holt slid off the stool, winking at Lydia. "Want to dance with me, Lyd? Cooper's giving us the death stare."

"God, yes," Lydia said, giving Steven the stink eye.

He watched them go, not sure what was awkward about the four of them chatting like every other night. "What the hell was that about?"

"No idea," Lauren said quickly, smoothing her dress over her tiny waist that he couldn't stop staring at. "Are we dancing, too?"

Steven's mouth watered, and he tugged on his bow tie, studying that spot where her waist flared out for her hips. He'd never been much of a hips guy, but something told him that his hand would fit perfectly right above there, right above her hot little ass — *shit*. There he went again. "Son of a bitch."

"It's just dancing." Lauren blinked and pursed her lips. He'd never noticed how delicious they were. All pink, and soft, and lush, and begging to be kissed. "Why are you looking at me like that? What's wrong?"

"Nothing." He stood and rolled his shoulders, shaking off his disturbing attraction to his best friend — *Lauren*, not Holt. He needed to knock this shit off. Cooper scowled at him and crooked his finger. He was the only Shillings guy not out there. Even Jake and Tara were with the team, laughing and looking as happy as pigs in shit. "Ready?"

She took a deep breath, curled her hands into fists, and nodded once. "Yeah. Sure."

Skimming his gaze down her slender form one last time, he held his arm out for her. She grabbed onto it with both hands, her body stiff against his. When she glanced at him out of the corner of her eye, she quickly turned away, blushing again. He couldn't help but wonder if she felt the same odd attraction as he did tonight — and if the whiskey was messing with her head as much as it was his.

This newfound desire might throw him off, but one thing was unchangeable. No matter how much he wanted her, or how badly he ached to see how those bare hips felt in his hands, or how soft those pink lips of hers really were, he wouldn't find out. Women like Lauren deserved all the happiness in the world.

Love. A family. A dog. A cat. A house.

A white motherfucking picket fence.

All the things *he* could never give her—so he wouldn't even try.

Chapter Two

The live orchestra played—she *loved* Mozart—and dancing couples swirled around them in fancy dresses and tuxedos, but all Lauren could see and hear was Steven Thomas. As he led her into the midst of the elegantly dancing crowd, his body hard and his arm even stiffer, she sensed an edginess in him that was stronger than ever before, and just as unattainable as he was.

He'd always been a restless man, moving quickly from one thing to another, never satisfied with life. She'd watched him go from woman to woman ever since he came back from his first tour in Iraq. Nothing was ever good enough, and she had yet to see him be happy with what he had. It was that same unquenchable drive that had sent him to the Navy, and right into a spot as a highly sought-after Navy SEAL.

Through it all, Lauren had been there.

Worrying. Waiting. Worrying. Watching. *Worrying.*

Yeah, worrying was mentioned three times. It should have been mentioned a thousand. Heck, a million. Through it all, no matter how far away he'd been, or what country he was in, she'd waited for him to call, write, or knock on her door.

So. Much. Waiting.

Sure, Lydia had been there, too. But she'd been young. Too young to understand what her brother was going through, and why he needed to disappear somewhere quiet whenever he came home. Lauren got it. She got *him*.

Always had.

He was slow to trust and even slower to care, but Lauren cared too much, too fast. Steven was heroic and brave and kind, while Lauren tended to hide in her shell when it came time to do something new. They were about as opposite as two people could possibly get...which made them awesome friends.

But tonight, she couldn't read him.

It was weird. And a little bit scary.

He was struggling to fit into society. To be normal, and a civilian, and all the things he hadn't been for years. And he'd been drinking too much lately. Lydia asked her to help. But she had no idea *how* to do that.

It wasn't as if she could command him to stop. He was a free man, and he had every right to sleep around if he chose to. And he did. Constantly.

Every girl he brought home was worse than the last one, and she hated them all. He was selling himself short, not letting himself get in a real relationship, and it hurt to watch him fall down the same hole, over and over again, and not be able to help him.

She glanced at him out of the corner of her eye, flushing when she caught him watching her as if...as if...*she* was the next woman on his list. But that didn't make any sense. He didn't want her. Never had. If he'd shown *any* signs of being attracted to her over the last twenty years, she would've noticed, thank you very much.

A girl didn't miss a man like Steven's attention.

He was devastatingly hot, in *so* many ways.

They reached the spot he picked out for them, and he turned to her, opening his arms. She slid into them, like she had a million times before. But tonight, when his hand closed around her waist, right above her hip, her breath caught in her throat. Not from the touch, but the darkness in his hazel eyes. That and his touch felt almost…possessive.

Which was stupid, really. Steven didn't think of her like *that*. "How's Brian?" He tightened his grip on her hip, focusing on her mouth.

"Uh…" She shrugged. "He's gone."

"Since when?"

"Since he slept with his secretary, like the cliché jerk he is," she said lightly. "I figured that was kind of a deal breaker for me."

"Kind of?" he growled. "I will never, in a million years, figure out why you continue to fall for the wrong type of guy, over and over again."

Probably something to do with the fact that the right guy, the guy she really wanted to be with, was off-limits. No matter how hard she tried, no other man lived up to Steven. They all came up short, in the end. So she'd stopped trying to find the right guy, and had fun with the wrong ones instead. "You know me."

"Yeah." Frowning down at her, he flexed his jaw. "I do."

They fell silent, and the air between them became charged. She couldn't figure out why, or how, but something was different tonight. Something *in* him. "Are you okay?"

His brows lowered, and his hand slid across her lower back. As it did so, he stepped closer, his nostrils flaring. Again, the touch felt as if he laid some sort of outdated claim over her. "Why would you ask me that?"

"You're acting…different." And it was messing with her head. Making her see things she had no right to. "Are you drunk again?"

"No."

"Okay…" She licked her lips. "Good."

"You're not going to start in on me, too, are you?" He leaned over her, placing his lips a breath away from her ear. "If you are, your love life is fair game to me, too. And I got a hell of a lot to say about that."

She swallowed hard and breathed in. His cologne filled her senses, awakening things that had long since been asleep. "Like what?"

Resting his chin on top of her head, he shrugged. "Like how you keep dating jerks, and how it's time you realized your self-worth. You deserve better."

The way he said that, all conviction and passion, made her heart skip a beat. It always did. He'd always been her best advocate, which just might be the worst thing. It was why she had yet to find a man who could live up to the standards he'd set back in fourth grade when he'd given her his only pencil in math class, so she wouldn't get in trouble for forgetting hers for the millionth time in a row.

She'd been screwed from that moment on.

"One could say the same of you," she argued, holding his hand tightly. "You deserve more than a one-night stand, and a thank-you pat on the butt in the morning."

Pulling back, he grinned in that lighthearted manner he always did. But he wasn't fooling her. She could see right through the bright veneer, and into the shadowy darkness he hid with jokes and charm. "I assure you that I deserve *exactly* what I'm getting."

His tone was joking, but his words weren't. He had it in his head that he was this horrible, bad guy, when he was the furthest thing from that. He was loyal, brave, kind, and selfless, but he was too damn stubborn to see, or admit, that.

She pressed her lips together. "Well, actually—"

He spun her in a circle without warning, pulled her into his chest, and grinned down at her when she clung to him, letting out a yelp. "Watch yourself, Brixton. Life loves to throw you for loops like that."

She hung on to his arm. "Or your best friend does."

"Exactly." He hugged her close, swaying to the music again. For the first time all night, he acted like himself. Like the "him" he was before he came home from war and took the position at Shillings Agency. "I'm a sick bastard like that."

"No kidding," she muttered. The song ended, and she went to move out of his arms. When he didn't let go of her, she looked at him in confusion. "What are you doing? Your boss saw you out here, so your obligatory dance is over."

His grin widened. "Let's dance again. I don't want to talk to anyone tonight, and I'm having fun."

"You're talking to me." She curled a hand behind his neck, the motion as natural as breathing or blinking. "Right now."

"Oh, cupcake." He locked gazes with her. "You don't count."

She tilted her head to the side. "I'm not sure whether to be insulted, or honored."

"Depends how you look at it, I suppose." He ran his thumb over the back of her hand. "Hey. Are you okay?"

"Yeah, why wouldn't I be?"

"Brian." He looked at her again, and this time, it was as if he saw right through her. "Are you upset?"

She shook her head, not breaking contact. Brian was nothing. She didn't care that he was gone, or that it was over. The only man who mattered to her was in her arms right now. "Of course. He was…he was just a distraction."

"From?"

Biting down on her tongue, she lifted a shoulder. "I don't know. Life?"

"I get that. Life can be a real bitch sometimes."

"Yeah." Lauren tightened her grip on his hand. "Are *you* okay?"

He cocked his head. "I already answered that."

Sure he did. But the thing with Steven was that he thought he hid his struggle to rejoin society from her—from everyone. He checked his surroundings all the time and he couldn't enter a crowded room without examining all corners for attack. And every time a loud bang surprised him, he instinctively reached for his gun...and then shortly after, a woman and a drink.

But she noticed. And she was worried for him.

"I think you lied."

"I'm not a liar," he said stiffly. He spun her in a circle again, catching her easily when she stumbled. His strong arms around her, holding her tight and safe, made her even more aware of the small amount of distance between them. "Even if everyone else in this damn world is."

"Not me," she said breathlessly. "I don't lie to you."

"And I don't lie to you. It's what makes us—us. But we're not fucking. If we were, it would be different. One of us would lie, and ruin things, and it would be over."

"That's an awfully bleak outlook on life...and us."

He lifted a shoulder. "It's true, though. Everyone lies in relationships, which is why I avoid them. When you're with someone, you have to pretend you're happy, or in love, even when you're not. Even if the only thing you're thinking about is how to get away from your girlfriend or boyfriend, because there's got to be more to life than *this*, you just keep smiling. Acting like you're happy. You know it as well as I do. When was the last time you felt like you really belonged in someone's arms?"

Right here. Right now. With you. "With a guy I was dating? Probably never."

"But you've felt that way before?" he asked, his voice low.

She bit her tongue, not sure how to answer. If she said yes, he'd ask who she felt that way about. And if he asked, she'd have to tell him the truth. But if she admitted out loud that he made her happy, and she felt complete in his arms...

There would be no taking that back.

And she had a feeling she wouldn't like his reaction.

"Does it matter? We're not talking about that. We were talking about sex and lies—two things which I don't associate with you," she said, hoping that would be enough to satisfy his curiosity. "Like, ever."

He laughed, and he stepped a little closer. Despite his laughter, he looked anything but amused. He looked... determined. His tallness and hard muscles crowded her, making her feel miniscule in comparison, and the way he watched her—all domineering, and full of sexual power and an unspoken challenge—made her stumble over her own two feet.

He, of course, caught her.

Just like he always did.

The heat of his touch burned her, and her stomach clenched tight. It filled her with an unanswered need that would never be satisfied by anyone but him.

Leaning down, he spoke low. His breath fanned over her cheeks, and she stiffened. "Come on, Lauren. Let's be honest. You've never, even once, thought about it? About what it would be like between us if we got stupid, naked, and sweaty? How good it might feel if I fucked you, hard and rough, against a wall, just for fun?"

Oh, crap. Now that would be *all* she could think about, thank you very much. "I...uh...well..."

Luckily, she was saved from answering. The song ended, and as soon as it did, Holt and Lydia came up, laughing and holding hands. "Can we switch partners?" Holt asked, nudging Lydia slightly. "She's sick of me already."

Steven studied Lauren, jaw ticking, and for a second, she thought he might refuse. But instead he grinned and turned to the other man, the carefree mask he wore so well slipping right back into place. "Sure, man. I figured it was only a matter of time till you were back in my arms again."

Holt snorted. "I think I'll take Lauren, if you don't mind."

"You're stuck with me, brother," Lydia said, twisting her lips. "Holt's mine now."

He let go of Lauren, squeezing her hand one last time. "I think that's a deal I can gladly accept. Holt sweats too much anyway. Come here."

Laughing, Lydia went into his arms. "He doesn't *sweat*."

Lauren watched them, smiling.

That was something she had never had. A family. A brother that loved her. Her own father had run away when she was a baby, and her mother hadn't had time for her as she grew up, since she'd been busy working three jobs to pay the bills. And then, when she was seventeen and a fresh graduate out of high school, her mother had committed suicide. Everyone who was supposed to love her had run away.

It was one of the reasons she didn't let people in.

Steven gave her one last, long, scorching glance. "We'll finish our conversation later."

She swallowed and watched him go, heart racing and palms sweating. What was *up* with him tonight? She glanced at Holt. He watched her skeptically. She shook her head. "Don't ask."

"I have a feeling it's none of my business, so I won't," he said, his voice soft. "He's different around you, though. Like a completely different guy."

She turned to him. "What do you mean?"

"You've known him a long time. A lot longer than I have."

"Yeah…" She moved into his arms and smiled up at him. He was attractive, in that hot, nerdy way. She had a feeling

Lydia hadn't stood a chance when they'd met. There was something about Holt that was irresistibly charming, and he had a way of making you like him with nothing more than a smile. "But he fought with you overseas. In some ways, you know him better than I ever will."

"We only crossed paths once or twice. Different branches." He shrugged. "But it was enough to learn what kind of man he is. I only really see him relax around you. When he was dancing with you just now, and laughing, it was like looking at a completely different guy. It's weird."

She sought out Steven. He chatted with Lydia, laughing, but Holt was right. He wasn't relaxed. He was tense. Alert. Aware. He kept glancing around the room, his gaze falling on Lauren every so often, as if making sure she was still there.

Holt cleared his throat. "He needs you. You make him happy."

"He has me," she said quickly, focusing on Holt again. He watched her seriously, as if he thought she might not mean it. "Always has."

Across the room, Steven laughed and kissed the top of Lydia's head, then walked toward the bar. Getting yet *another* drink. It's all he did lately. Maybe she *should* try and come up with a way to help him. To get him to see why he wasn't really making it better.

Why he needed to focus on the good things in his life...

And stop drowning himself in the bad.

Chapter Three

Three hours later, Steven walked down Main Street alone, passing the laundromat with a shiver, and cursed the cold Maine night air. Even in summer, once the sun went down, the cold took over and chased away all signs of warmth and brightness. Why he hadn't moved to a tropical paradise by now, he had no fucking clue. But he remembered the three reasons he stayed in this godforsaken place.

Lydia. Holt. And *Lauren*.

Damn. He still couldn't get Lauren out of his head. Had to be the booze.

His phone buzzed, and he pulled it out. He stumbled a bit, the drink he'd pounded back before leaving hitting him. After that last one, he almost brought a brunette that slightly reminded him of Lauren home with him. Almost tried to pretend she was Lauren, so he could bang her out of his system, so to speak.

But that inner voice hadn't been quieted by booze yet, and he left before he uttered the words that would have him hating himself come morning.

Catching himself before he hit the sidewalk, he squinted down at his phone. Recognizing the name immediately, he swiped his finger across the screen. A taxi had dropped Lauren off at her place an hour ago, before he'd had it leave him at another bar. What did she need, this late?

"Long time, no see."

"It's me." She paused, and added, "Lauren."

"Yeah. I see that." He glanced at his phone again. "It's after midnight. Why the hell are you still awake?"

She breathed heavily. "I just got out of the shower, and I hear something out in my living room. Footsteps."

He gripped the phone tightly. He couldn't drive, but he had legs—and he could sure as hell haul ass to her place. "Lock the door. I'll be there in ten."

"Thanks."

The numbing effect of the whiskey was gone, and his stomach churned with fear he wouldn't make it to her in time. That something would happen to her…and he'd fucking lose it. He hung up and glanced up at the street sign, then took off, full speed.

As he ran, he tried to slip into a battle-like calm, a mask he wore all too well. It didn't work. There was no calming down— not when Lauren was in danger. He'd fought insurgents, ISIS agents, and every kind of monster one could imagine.

But someone hurting Lauren?

It was unlike anything he'd ever experienced before. It made him want to hurl, shoot someone, pound his chest, and scream in agony—all at the same time.

It made him lose his motherfucking mind.

He reached her road in record time, his breathing still even and labored, as he counted it off in his head. Brick exterior. Four concrete stairs. Wrought iron railing and window bars. Lauren's red Mazda he'd helped her buy. To thank him, she'd made him his favorite cupcakes. Red velvet.

He took the stairs two at a time, and turned the knob. It didn't budge. Backing up, he was just about to throw himself into the damn door when it swung inward. His breath caught in his throat for the second time that night. When he'd first met her as a kid, he'd thought she was the most beautiful girl he'd ever seen.

After all these years, and lots of women, his opinion hadn't changed.

She wore a tiny blue towel. There were no visible bruises or cuts. Her bright blue eyes were wide and she breathed heavily, clinging to the towel with white knuckles. Her dark brown hair was still damp from the shower, and she was devoid of makeup. She bit down on her trembling lower lip—soft, pink lips that were more tempting than he'd ever imagined possible—and watched him. "It's okay. I'm okay."

She's okay.

Breathing easily for the first time since he hung up that damn phone, he yanked her into his arms and hugged her, incapable of even trying to resist. She'd scared the shit out of him, and he needed to make sure she was okay. Needed to *feel* it. Her small frame only reached his chest, reminding him why he called her cupcake. Her size and her fondness for baking— hell, she even owned a small bakery in town now that she was all grown up—had sealed that years ago. But tonight she seemed smaller. More frail.

He would die to protect her.

But first, he had to find out what he was protecting her *from*.

He breathed in her sweet cupcake scent one last time. Letting go of her, he gave her what he hoped was a small, reassuring smile, and asked, "What happened? Did anyone actually—" He cut off. A few lamps were knocked over, and a broken vase lay on the floor. "Shit. I'm calling the cops."

Her lower lip trembled again, and she shook her head.

"Don't."

"What the hell do you mean, *don't*?"

"When I heard the crash, at first I thought it was Loki. But I heard the footsteps, and I panicked. That's when I called you. But then the front door closed, and he was gone, so I came out. And stuff was missing."

He frowned at the cat in question, which sat licking his paw and staring at him with condescension. That creature hated him. He was sure of it. "Then why the hell aren't we calling the cops?"

She shifted on her feet. He got the distinct impression she was hiding something from him, or maybe even lying, but he wasn't sure. He wasn't even sure she had a tic. But she knew how he felt about liars. It *had* to be something else. "I don't want them here. I want you."

He blinked, feeling like he was in some sort of fucked up twilight zone. "Why?"

"Because…I…" She covered her face. "I think it was Brian. He took a few things, but they were all his, so there's no real crime to report. He snuck in while I was in the shower, and left."

"Why didn't he just knock?" He tugged her hands down and studied her beautiful face—trying his best not to picture her naked and wet in the shower. It was like trying to outrun an erupting volcano, though. Sooner or later, you were going to get burned. "Why would he sneak in like a thief while you were showering?"

She hesitated. "Well, we didn't exactly end on the best terms."

"Yeah. He slept with his secretary."

"And he…he was jealous of you." She glanced at Steven, but quickly lowered her head. "Maybe he saw us together earlier, and got angry. He probably knocked, but when I didn't answer, he came in and got his stuff. Maybe he didn't even think I was home."

He tightened his hold on her. Her skin was so soft and smooth—the opposite of his hardened, calloused palms. His hands had done things she'd never even be able to imagine. And yet she'd stuck by him. And the idea that he was somehow responsible for the break-in...he didn't like the way it made him feel. "Why would he be jealous of *me*? We're just friends. Strictly platonic."

Except lately, he didn't feel platonic.

He felt horny as hell.

"I..." She cleared her throat. "I don't know why."

They stared at each other, neither moving. Her tits rose and fell with each breath, and no matter how hard he tried, his gaze kept returning to her abundant cleavage.

After a few moments, Steven cleared his throat. He couldn't stop thinking about what she would do if he kissed her. So, instead, he walked over to a lamp and picked it up, setting it in place. Mostly to put distance between them before he did something stupid. "So you're not scared anymore?"

"I wouldn't say that." She hesitated. "I don't think we need to call the cops on the guy, but it did freak me out. And... and...I don't want to be alone."

That, he got. It was the first time she made sense since he walked in the door. Something was off. He couldn't place his finger on what, or why, but it was. "You want me to hang out?"

"Yeah." She lifted her lashes. When she did, it made his blood heat and his heart speed up. "Can you stay with me for a few days? Please? I don't want to be alone if he comes back, and I need you. With me."

Stay...with her?

For *days*?

He'd spent the night before. Slept on the couch. Hell, they'd even slept in the same bed together once or twice. But to spend *days* with her, and only her, when his brain was all fucked up? That was asking for trouble. "Why so long?"

She didn't answer, her bright blue eyes filling with tears, wringing her hands in front of her. "Steven…" she whispered, her voice soft. "*Please*."

He held his arms open, holding back all the questions he had about her odd request and her even stranger behavior. When she was ready to talk, she would. "Of course I'll stick around. Come here."

Without hesitation, she threw herself into his arms and held on tight, her entire body melding to his flawlessly. "Thank you."

"Anytime." He rested his cheek on the top of her head. "You know that."

She didn't answer. Just held on to him even tighter.

He could count on one hand the amount of times he'd seen Lauren this worked up over something, in all of the twenty years they'd been friends. Something had her worried as hell, and he was dying to figure out what that something was, but he'd be here for her until it was better. Or until she was ready to talk about it. Or both.

Tightening his hold on her, he kissed the top of her head. "Shh. It's all right. You're all right. I'm here. I'll stay."

She nodded as he spoke, obviously needing the words, so he kept saying them. After a while, he stopped paying attention to what he said. He was too busy rubbing her back and smoothing her hair back from her damp face. She smelled like vanilla and sugar cookies—and for the first time in a while…

He felt like he belonged somewhere.

Slowly, she lifted her face to his. The force of their gazes colliding was strong enough to send the entire solar system out of orbit. "You have no idea how much I need you, Steven. You're the one person I can always count on."

His heart wrenched painfully to the left before centering

itself again. "The feeling is mutual." He rested his cheek on the top of her head. "And anytime you need me, I'm here, no matter how silly you might think it is."

She nodded, sniffed, and let go of him. "Okay."

He reluctantly did the same, letting her step back. His arms felt empty the second he did so. Until she sniffed and swiped her hands over her cheeks, he hadn't even realized she'd been crying. Lauren *never* cried. He stepped forward again, gaze locked on her. "Damn it, cupcake. Tell me what's wrong so I can fix it."

"I'm fine." Once she studied him, she let a little laugh out. It sounded hoarse and forced. "I got you all wet."

She wasn't fine, but no amount of pestering would force her to tell him what was on her mind. So he'd bide his time, and do his best to distract her from whatever was messing with her head. "Hey. That's usually my line."

Lauren gasped, her cheeks going pink. "*Steven.*"

"Sorry. Couldn't resist." Steven laughed and shook out his damp shirt. "I mean, you practically handed it to me on a silver platter."

"Yeah, I did, didn't I?" She grabbed a tissue, shaking her head as she walked into her bedroom. "Give me a second to throw some clothes on."

He nodded. Clothes were definitely a good idea. "I'll be right here."

Smiling, she shut the door. When she came out a minute or two later, she wore a skimpy pair of pajamas that barely covered her ass. "I thought you were getting dressed," he said drily.

"I did." She glanced down with a wrinkled brow. "I'm going to have a drink. You're not getting one. You had enough earlier."

"Yes, mother." He followed her, dragging a hand through his hair as he watched her walk. She was always so graceful.

Even when rocked by something strong enough to make her cry, she managed to keep her beauty and grace with each step she took. "I didn't want one anyway."

"Too much already?" she asked, peeking over her shoulder at him.

Lifting a shoulder, he leaned against the entrance to the kitchen. "Maybe. Maybe not. I'll tell you in the morning."

Instead of laughing, as he'd expected, she frowned, way too somber for his own liking. She watched him as if she knew all his deepest, darkest secrets...and didn't judge him one little bit. But she didn't. Couldn't. He went to great lengths to hide how messed up he was from everyone.

Especially her.

She turned away and lifted the lid off the glass container in her kitchen, and he let out a sigh of relief. It had cupcakes in it. It always did. As if owning a bakery wasn't enough for her, she also felt the need to bake at home. It was her way of self-soothing.

He drank and fucked. She baked things.

Not all that different, really.

"Do you ever worry you don't have your life as together as you might hope?" she asked, her voice distracted and shaky. "That every choice you make is only messing it up even more, until it's a tangled mess you'll never recognize?"

"Every damn day," he admitted, even though he didn't want to. But he refused to lie to her, even if he couldn't stand the idea of her discovering he wasn't the strong, resilient man she thought he was. The type of guy she could call on nights like these.

Even if he could never call her his.

Chapter Four

When someone broke into her house while she was naked in the shower, and scared half a year off of her life, obviously the first person Lauren called had been Steven. And when the door shut behind her intruder, and she poked her head out, and the only stuff missing had been the stuff she laid out for Brian…

Yeah, she'd put two and two together pretty quickly.

But by then Steven was at her door, and about to come in, and she'd had little to no time to recover from the scare. And when he'd hugged her tight, concern etched all across his handsome face…an idea had come to her.

One that, once planted, had been impossible to ignore.

Earlier, she wished there was a way to make sure he was okay. To make him remember the good things in his life. This was the opportune chance to do that, up close and personal. If he thought she was still scared, or was shaken up, he would never leave her side. It would give her the opportunity to remind him how fun life could be…

If you were with the right person.

So she rolled with it. Maybe she over-acted on some points, but it had worked. He was here, and she was here, and now all she needed was a game plan of fun.

But despite her excitement at this opportunity, she couldn't ignore one cold, hard fact: for the first time in their relationship, she lied to him. And if he found out...

God, he could *never* find out.

She, more so than anyone, understood his hatred of liars. It stemmed from childhood, when his parents had lied about being happy but had been sleeping with other people behind each other's backs, and continued throughout his adult years. It continued when his one and only girlfriend as an adult had done the same thing to him.

He couldn't abide lies of any kind.

She'd seen him walk away from friendships over them.

Up until a few moments ago, Lauren hadn't had a reason to worry. Now, she did. It was a small lie. More a lie by omission than anything else. Brian *had* come in, and she *had* been scared...for a second or two. She took a deep breath, staring down at the red velvet cupcakes with cream cheese frosting and red sprinkles as if they held the secrets of the world. They didn't. She'd know, since she'd made them. They were just cupcakes, and she was just her, and Steven was just...

Steven was just *Steven*.

Her best friend.

Glancing at him over her shoulder, she took a deep breath. His reddish blond hair—he'd lecture her for calling it that, because it was too feminine, and according to him it was just *red*—and hazel eyes were topped off by loyalty, dedication, selflessness, strength, and a hell of a six-pack. The rest of his muscles matched that toned abdomen of his, all the way down to his huge...

Well, really, tight boxers only hid so much.

Especially on a guy as big as Steven.

She'd never been as fond of underwear as she had been the first day he came out of her bathroom, wearing nothing but a whole lot of damp skin and form-fitting black boxers. It had been a sight pretty enough to wake the dead. Maybe that was how the zombie apocalypse would come. Steven in a pair of boxers…walking through a cemetery.

That was part of being friend-zoned—he stripped down to his boxers in front of her as if she didn't count as a woman at all. Sometimes, she thought he forgot she *was* one. He certainly didn't treat her like one.

Not that she *wanted* him to, of course.

She was all too aware that he went through women faster than she went through sugar, and she didn't exactly have the best track record either. Take her habit of falling too fast and too hard, add a pinch of his promiscuity and inability to commit, and they'd be an undeniable recipe for disaster and heartbreak.

She knew it. He did, too. Or at least, she assumed he did.

They'd never actually talked about it…until tonight, when he'd asked her if she ever thought about the two of them. About what it would be like. She had. Lots.

But she'd never *admit* it out loud.

So what if she'd never find out what it was like to have Steven look at her as if he needed her more than he needed air, or water, or life itself? That was a *good* thing.

Or so she kept telling herself anyway.

Plastering on a smile, she turned to him. "Cupcake?"

"Of course." He smiled and took it. He always did. "Thanks."

When he took the treat, his fingers brushed hers as he tugged it out of her hand, and Lauren clenched her jaw at the inevitable rush of lust that swept through her veins at the touch. That was nothing new. Her inability to ignore it, however, was.

She blamed his odd behavior from earlier tonight.

Giving him her back, she pulled out a shot glass. She could still smell the whiskey on Steven. She probably ruined the second part of his evening when she called, but for some reason, she wasn't sorry. She poured a shot of rum and tossed it back, shuddering at the burn.

He chewed on his cupcake contemplatively, watching her closely as she immediately poured another, and tossed that one back, too. When she poured a third, he shook his head. "Lauren."

"I'm fine. Just one more, and I'll be good."

Steven made a disgruntled sound and covered her hand with his. Gently, he pried the bottle out of her hands. His hand was warm and calloused, and it made her want to ignore the voices in her head for once. To take what she wanted. *Him.*

Always had. Always would.

"I don't know what's wrong, but I'm not about to watch you drink a whole damn bottle of rum." He eyed her with concern. "That won't help you with anything."

She forced a smile. "It works for you, right?"

"No." He flexed his jaw. "It doesn't."

She tossed back the shot she'd poured before he took it away, too. Of course, he faced away from her to set the bottle back on the counter, so he missed it, but *she* didn't miss the way his navy pants hugged his rear to perfection. Screw Superman. This man had buns of steel. Maybe if she told him that, he would push her against a wall and follow through on—oh, crap.

The alcohol was giving her bad, *bad* thoughts.

Since she couldn't stop staring at his butt, she turned around and faced the wall, gripping the counter so hard her knuckles ached. "Then why do you keep doing it? And why can't I? What makes us any different?"

"Drinking to drown your worries and fears only makes

everyone else worry about you more. And it makes me—"
He broke off, cursing under his breath. "I...you...*shit*. Your
drinking was all to show me I'm being an idiot and making
you worry all the time, isn't it?"

Not turning around, she lifted a shoulder. "Ding ding
ding."

When he came up behind her, his Hugo Boss cologne
washed over her, and the heat of his body touched hers. He
was so big and hard and comforting, and she was *this close* to
throwing herself into his arms and never letting go...

Screw the consequences.

"Well played."

A smile lifted the corner of her mouth. "Point?"

"Yours," he said, his tone begrudging. "But what did I tell
you at the party?"

*That you were going to throw me up against a wall and
take me roughly?* "Uh..."

"If you want to talk about my drinking?" Gently, he
turned her around and rested his hand on her shoulder. The
other reached out and brushed her hair out of her face. "Then
your love life is fair game, too."

His sweet touch, paired with his soft voice, and the way
he looked at her as if she meant a whole lot more to him than
she should, warred with his strong and possessive hold on her
shoulder. The contrast did *things* to her it shouldn't. Things
that were a heck of a lot harder to ignore with two and a half
shots of rum in her belly.

What was *wrong* with her?

She licked her lips. "Well, then, by all means. Speak."

"Oh, I will." He moved even closer, his gaze locked on her
mouth. Why was the urge to close her eyes and lift her face to
his so strong? "Are you scared?"

Terrified, actually. But not of what he might say. She was
scared of the feelings coming to life inside of her. They were

strong, and real, and they wouldn't go away. For just a night, she wanted him, to *be* with him, and she didn't care if it was a bad idea.

He glanced down, watching the path her tongue left, and took a small step closer. "Brian was a douche, and so was every guy before him. You keep dating men who don't deserve you, and it pisses me the hell off."

Her heart sped up. He studied her with a heat that could only be explained in one way. He quickly shook it off and gave her the same tender smile he always did, the one that said he thought of her as a sister, or a bro, and nothing more. "Funny, so do you."

"I don't date at all. I fuck."

She bit down on her tongue. "I do that, too. Just more than once with the same guy. You should try it sometime."

For a second, it looked like he might say something meaningful. Like admit that the reason he didn't date was that he was scared to open himself up like that, or that he didn't think he deserved love and commitment. But then he grinned, and the somberness in his eyes gave way to laughter. "Try fucking a guy? Well, they say you never know till you give it a good old college try…but I'll pass. I like chicks, not dicks."

"That's not what I meant," she said, frowning.

"What do you want me to say? That I'll go out and fall in love with some girl?" He gritted his teeth so hard there was a grinding sound. "I tried that once already, with Rachel, and it didn't work out so well."

She nodded. "Yeah. She cheated on you. That doesn't mean every other woman out there will, too."

"Funny, considering most of your asshole boyfriends *have*."

Sucking in a breath, she blinked. "That was harsh."

"Shit. I'm sorry." He blew out a breath and met her eyes.

"I didn't mean to say that."

"Yeah. You did." She lifted a shoulder. "And it's true. Ever since the day I was born, guys love to leave me, or cheat on me, or both. History doesn't lie."

"The only way I'd walk away from you was if they carried me away in a coffin," he said, his voice low. "I would never leave you."

She couldn't tell if he was saying he'd never leave her—as a friend—or if he was insinuating she should give him a chance to be *more*. When he lowered his hand from her cheek, she caught it, holding on tight. And nothing short of a tornado whipping through her kitchen would make her let go. "Steven…"

He swallowed hard, and his fingers flexed in hers, that heat still burning behind those warm hazel depths of his. "Yeah?"

Sucking in a deep breath, she rested her hand on his heart. It raced beneath her palm, speeding up even more when she locked gazes with him. There it was again. The heat she'd just sworn she would never see in his eyes. "You're *everything* to me. And I…I want…"

Instead of finishing her sentence, she went with it.

She let the booze guide her actions.

Lifting up on her tiptoes, she pressed her lips to his. And it felt as amazing as she always thought it would. The second their mouths touched, it was like she finally made the right choice, which was insane. She knew herself, and Steven. And yet…

It felt *right*.

For a second, his mouth pressed back against hers, and his grip on her tightened. He groaned and took over the kiss, closing his arms around her tightly. This was *it*. The moment she'd been waiting for. The *man* she'd been waiting for. Steven Thomas.

A moan escaped her, and he froze, his mouth still glued to

hers. With a harsh movement, he jerked back, a scowl marring his face, and his mouth pressed tightly into a line. "What the fuck, Lauren?"

Pressing her hand to her mouth, she stared back at him. And had no clue what to say.

Chapter Five

Steven had no damn clue what the hell was going on, but she didn't really mean that kiss. Throughout all the years they'd shared as friends, all the drinks they'd drunk together, and the numerous times they'd shared a bed—she'd never once done *that*.

She was drunk, upset about something she refused to dig into, and doing things she hadn't fully thought through. Doing anything to forget whatever it was that upset her in the first place. With any other girl, in any other place, he could be her guy.

Pressing her fingers to her mouth, she shook her head quickly. Those tiny little pajamas she always wore to bed taunted him more than they had before the kiss, and he'd never been so damn aware of how much skin those shorts left bare on her legs before now. "I'm sorry. I thought…I…"

When she didn't finish, he crossed his arms. "You thought you could use me to forget whatever you're upset about?"

"N-No. It's just I'm alone, and you're alone…and it's quiet. So quiet. And when you looked at me like you were thinking about—"

A horrible thought occurred to him. One that made him sick with anger and…and…fuck it, he might as well admit it. *Jealousy*. So much damn jealousy he might as well turn green and start smashing shit with his fist. "Jesus, Lauren. Is this about Brian? Do you miss him so badly you had to use me to fill a void?"

Her jaw dropped. "What? *No*."

No matter what had caused this kiss to occur, it hadn't been her overwhelming desire for him. That was what pissed him off the most about this.

She wasn't kissing him because she *wanted* to, or even because she wanted *him*. She was using him to forget something, and now their first kiss was wasted. There had been times where he pictured kissing her. Where he forgot why he never could, and got lost in the moment. Over the years, he imagined kissing her in tons of ways.

On the beach at sunset. In a fancy restaurant. At his place, after he cooked dinner for her and they shared the dessert she made for them. She'd have icing on her lip, and he'd lean in to wipe it off, smiling. Their eyes would meet, and suddenly… it would just happen. And it would have been everything he never knew he wanted.

But never *once* had he ever imagined their first kiss being like *this*.

A drunken ploy to forget another man.

It should have been tender. Loving. Kind. Passionate. "Tell me the truth. Do you miss him? Is it a way to forget what is so very obviously bothering you?"

She dropped her hand to her side, and her lower lip trembled. "No. *No*. I wasn't using you to try to forget about him, or anything."

"Then why?" he asked, trying to keep his tone non-accusatory, but failing miserably. "Why did you kiss me? Why now?"

Cheeks pinking, she advanced on him. "In that moment, it felt like I needed to, and have for a long time, you idiot. Do I need more of a reason than that?"

His heart raced faster than a speeding bullet. "Bullshit."

"No. It's. Not." She shoved him, both hands on his chest, but he didn't budge. She used about as much force as a mouse fighting off a cat would. "I needed to…to feel…and you *always* make me feel. You're always there, and I…I…*kissed* you. I picked the right guy for once, and I'd do it all over again."

He swallowed hard. He'd never denied her anything she asked him, but this was entering dangerous territory. This was *bad*. "You're drunk. You have no idea what you're saying right now."

Shaking her head, she stepped back from him. He felt the distance all the way to his dark fucking soul. "Not drunk enough to forget what I want, or to mistake what I'm feeling here." She pressed a hand to her stomach. "I want you, Steven. *You*."

Shit, he'd love to believe she spoke from the heart, rather than the bottle. But he watched her pound back the booze, and her tolerance was nonexistent. She was drunk off her ass, and nothing she said could be held accountable right now. Not even if he longed to kiss her again. Now that he had a taste, he couldn't think of anything else he would like more. "*Lauren*."

Her brows drew in. "Don't. Don't look at me like that."

"Like what?" he asked.

"Like you didn't like it." She threw a pointed glance southward. "You did."

His dick hardened even more, all because she looked at him. *Pull your shit together down there, man.* "We shouldn't have done that. We should forget—"

"*No*." She fisted her hands, her chest rising and falling rapidly. "Don't say it. If you do, I swear to God I'll make you regret it."

He steadied himself with one long breath. He was going to say it, no matter what she threatened. It *needed* to be said, for the sake of their friendship. It was like he stood on the edge of a cliff, and one small push from her would send him plummeting to his death…or his salvation. Damned if he could tell which one. "You should go to bed. We'll pretend this never happened, and—"

Snarling, she threw herself at him, her mouth catching his for the second time that night. And this time…he didn't push her away. There was no way in hell he could manage to reject her twice in one night. Not in this universe.

Hell, not even if he relived this moment every single day for a hundred years, with the express purpose of having a chance to choose differently. Even then, every *single* time, he would pull her closer.

He swept her into his arms and kissed her, letting all the frustration, confusion, and desire he felt wash out through that kiss. Sharing all the mixed up emotions he held close to his chest, and more. He backed her against the wall, his hands cradling her face as he ravaged her mouth, not letting his inner conscience have a say. Not right now. Maybe not ever.

She tasted and felt like salvation…

And damn it all to hell, he needed to be *saved*.

Moaning, she clung to him tightly, and opened her mouth under his. He didn't hesitate to take advantage of that. Didn't even pause to acknowledge what a horrible idea this was. He'd just give her what she needed…

Like he always did.

Sliding his hands under her ass, he lifted her up and stepped between her thighs, and she locked her legs around him tightly without any sign of the hesitation or doubt *he* couldn't ignore. The second he pressed against her wet heat, he was a lost man.

Or maybe he was found.

After this, there would be no going back for him. No more pretending he didn't notice how pretty she was, or how much she made him laugh, or how she was one of the only people who truly understood him. The one person he trusted. For years, he did his best to ignore the fact that she was everything, and more. Refused to even consider that she might be the reason he hadn't settled down with anyone, and ignored everyone when they said that very thing.

All this time, he laughed it off and treated the notion of him and Lauren as if it was an impossible theory, and so had she. But now that he had her in his arms...

It didn't feel so impossible after all. Nothing did. He felt like he was king of the world, and she was his queen. And that was bad. *Real* bad.

She deserved better than a guy like him.

Shutting his thoughts off, he rolled his hips against her, digging his fingers into the sides of her ass. She was wet and hot and sweet — and he could easily get lost in her. In *this*. She groaned into his mouth, her nails digging into his shoulders through his thin dress shirt. Slowly, he ran his hands up her sides, learning her curves.

He gripped the spot where her hips flared out gently from her tiny waist, curling his hands in that small spot possessively. Perfect. Just as he'd fantasized earlier. She rocked against him, small sexy sounds escaping her as she did so. When he moved his hands up her flat stomach, under the flimsy tank top she wore, and closed them over her tits, she writhed in his arms. She didn't have a bra on.

God help them both.

Groaning, he skimmed the tips of his thumbs across her perky nipples. She fit in his hands perfectly, filling his palms and spilling out a little. He deepened the kiss as he learned her body in new ways — ways he'd never imagined *actually* coming to life.

Her hands drifted down his back and over his shoulders, where she fisted his shirt. She urged him closer, like she couldn't get enough, and pushed against his hard, aching dick. This kiss, this moment, was something he couldn't express with mere words. It's like the whole world shifted and changed, all because he kissed Lauren.

And the thing was, it didn't feel like a bad change.

Rolling her nipples in between his fingers and thumbs, he tugged and rocked his hips into her, cursing the clothes that kept him from plunging inside her warm depths once and for all. Gliding his hands down her smooth skin, he cupped her ass, learning the feel of it in his hands. It felt like fucking heaven.

Like she belonged in his arms.

She cried out, arching her back and rolling her hips in a figure eight motion. She dug her heels into his lower back impatiently. Her urgency was a tangible thing, and she was close to the edge. All she needed was a little push. He could give her that, at least.

Breaking off the kiss, he bit down on her shoulder and thrust against her again, letting his hard dick hit her clit. She moaned and moved against him frantically, letting go of his shirt to bury her hands in his hair. Tugging, she lifted his head till they were nose- to-nose, looked him in the eyes, and said, "I need you to make me come now."

And then she kissed him.

Something inside of him snapped. There was no controlled seduction. No slow, easy moves meant to tease her and draw her higher. She wanted him to make her come? Well, then, she'd get it. No games. No teasing. Just orgasms.

Whatever she asked for, he gave her.

That wouldn't change now.

Sliding his hand lower, he pressed his thumb against her clit, cursing the material that kept him from touching her flesh, and traced a circle around it. She tensed in his arms, and she came. That easily. It was as if she'd been waiting for years to get off, and now that he finally gave her a chance, she wasn't going to waste time.

It was a big turn-on.

She tore her mouth free and dropped her head back against the light yellow wall, a small, strangled sound escaping her. Her breathing went ragged and harsh, and she collapsed against the wall, her chest heaving. He'd barely touched her, but she was already quivering from the orgasm he'd given her. "*Steven.*"

He'd never been so moved by another person's pleasure before.

Slowly, he removed his hand from between her legs, his heart pounding so loudly all he could hear was its erratic beats. "That might be the fastest a man's ever gotten a woman off before," he said drily. "Do I get a gold medal?"

A small laugh escaped her, and she blew her hair out of her face. "I apparently needed that."

He laughed too, and that's when it hit him.

The reason she affected him so much, so deeply, was because he cared about her. She was his best friend, she was drunk, and if he continued on this path that they were just starting on...

He was going to lose her.

She deserved courtship, roses, and romance. Not drinking, nightmares, and a one-night stand with her best friend. Gently, he lowered her to the floor, letting go of her once she steadied herself on her own two feet, even though it was the hardest thing he'd ever done before. "Lauren... Jesus."

She was willing and hot and sexy, and finally his. But he'd end up hurting her.

He had to stop.

Cheeks suffused with color, her mouth parted, and she

whispered, "Screw medals, Steven." The way she said his name, like she wasn't sure if she should thank him or curse him for eternity, rocked him to his core even more than her kisses had. "Instead, you get this."

She caught his mouth frantically, her tongue sweeping into his mouth this time. Her fingers fumbled with his fly. It was now or never. If he was going to end this before she did something she might regret, he had to move now. One more minute in her arms would be too much.

One more minute, and he wouldn't be able to walk away...

Cursing inwardly, he broke off the kiss, catching both her hands with one of his. For the first time ever, he was going to deny her something she wanted. "No."

She froze immediately. "No?"

"No." Bracing himself, he stepped back, still holding her hands. Stopping this before he discovered how sweet her body would feel, naked and entwined with his, was like holding a gun to his own hand and pulling the trigger. And just as painful. "This ends here. Go to bed before we do something we'll both regret. I'll take the couch."

She ripped her hands out of his. "I...I...I don't understand. Was it something I did?"

"No. I just—" He shoved his hands into his pockets to keep himself from reaching out and touching her. Kissing her. Taking her. It would be so easy. Turning her down would leave him with blue balls and a hard dick for a year—*at least*. "I can't do this."

"I..." She shook her head. "What have I done?"

And then she bolted for her bedroom.

He flinched when her bedroom door slammed shut behind her. She might be pissed at him now, but she'd thank him in the morning. He was sure of it.

Guys like him were always a regret when the sun came up.

Chapter Six

Sometime before dawn, Lauren woke up with a headache and blurry vision. No big shocker there. She rarely drank, and she'd pounded back a few shots within moments of one another on an empty stomach, all to prove a point.

Like an idiot.

She threw herself at Steven and he *refused* her. Sure, he made her come before sending her to her room alone, but still. He could've had her, and he chose to push her away instead. Refused to take her to bed.

He didn't want her like that.

Now, she was going to have to act as if it didn't hurt that he would sleep with virtually *any* other woman besides *her*. It did hurt. *A lot.*

Groaning, she rolled over and squinted at the clock. It was almost five o'clock in the morning, and right beyond that door, Steven slept peacefully on her couch. In the brightness of the morning, he would still be there. Waiting. Watching.

Knowing he could have had her, and hadn't.

Well, she'd gone and done it. Ruined years of platonic

friendship with a few sips of rum, and a misplaced, ill-timed, unwelcome kiss. What was she supposed to do now? Go out there, and pretend last night had never happened like he suggested? Even though her body *still* hummed from the orgasm he'd given her? He had been, hands down, the best she ever had.

And she hadn't even *had* him.

So not fair.

Tossing the pillow aside, she threw her legs over the side of the mattress and padded across the tan Berber carpet her landlord had just put in. If she had any hope of being able to deal with what was coming in the morning, she needed to pop a few Ibuprofen, and down a big glass of ice cold water.

She headed into the bathroom and brushed her teeth to wash away the taste of rum. Afterward, she opened the cabinet for some Ibuprofen…then remembered it was in the kitchen. She'd taken some last night when she'd come home from work.

"*Crap.*"

She crossed her bedroom and then cracked the door open, sliding through and tiptoing toward the living room. Halfway there, she froze. The TV was still on, and Steven was still awake. He sat on the couch, facing the TV, and held a glass of something dark. His hair stuck up all over the place, as if he'd been running his hands through it. He did that when he was stressed, or upset, and this time…

It was her fault.

She didn't even dare to breathe, one foot still frozen in the air. It wasn't too late to turn around and go back in her room. To pretend she hadn't seen him looking so upset. But this was Steven, and he was the most important person in the world to her, and he was probably worried she would hate him now…

And she couldn't *do* that to him.

His head dropped back against the couch. "Lauren," he

groaned, his tone strained.

Hugging herself, she took a deep breath and walked around the corner of the couch. "Look, I'm sorry about—"

The words choked her and turned into a gasp.

She'd noticed he was awake, but she hadn't seen was what he was *doing*. But, oh my God, she did now. Every. Single. Detail.

He sat on the couch, with his dress shirt unbuttoned. If not for what he was doing, she easily could have gotten caught up in his hard pecs, and even harder abs. And the light dusting of reddish blond hair on his chest was enthralling.

There was no other word for it.

Except maybe...addictive.

But the real show was taking place further south. His navy blue, pleated khakis were unbuttoned and unzipped, and his huge cock jutted out, erect and wanting, and his hand had been moving up and down the hard length with a strength that she couldn't look away from. Or ever forget. And, even though she should, she—

Oh my God, she couldn't look away.

Nothing could make her.

He froze mid-pump. She probably should have turned away, or covered her eyes, but she was too busy staring at his impressive length, and the long blue vein that ran up the side of his shaft. His large hand still held on to his huge erection, and his jaw hung open, as if he didn't have a clue what to say.

Neither did she.

She'd *literally* just caught him with his cock in his hand.

So she just stared. And stared some more. *My God*.

"Well." Swallowing so hard his Adam's apple bobbed, he straightened. "This isn't awkward or anything," he said drily.

"Y-You... I..." She finally covered her face. "Oh my God. Seriously? On my *couch*? I just bought it!"

The rustling of fabric as he tucked his erection away was

the only sound.

She peeked through her fingers. He didn't look any less hard. As far as she could tell, if anything, he seemed even harder than before she'd walked in. "It was either that, or in your bed. I figured you'd prefer the former."

"*You* obviously did." And just like that, the embarrassment and shock gave way to anger. A couple of hours ago, she offered herself up to him, and he refused. Made her feel like he didn't want her, or find her attractive, when he obviously did. And now he took what could have been—no, *should* have been—hers. "Was that supposed to...to...hurt me?"

"I'm sorry, I don't follow." He blinked, standing up unsteadily. He set down his glass, sloshing it over the side and onto her table. "How the hell is me jerking off a direct insult to you, when you weren't even supposed to see it, or find out it happened at all?"

He stood there like some sort of untamed sex god, with his pants undone, his cock hard, and his shirt open. All mussed hair and sex. And it wasn't *fair*. None of this was fair. "You let me think you didn't want me. Let me go to bed alone, ashamed that I threw myself at you, when you clearly weren't attracted to me. And the whole time, you're out here...doing *that*."

"I assure you I wasn't jacking off for hours." A muscle in his jaw ticked, and he drove his hand through his hair. "I was just trying to sleep, and I couldn't. I couldn't stop thinking about earlier. So I decided to ease a need that wouldn't shut the hell up so I could finally get some shut-eye. That's it."

She stomped up to him and smacked his shoulder. He didn't even flinch. It, of course, didn't hurt him. The man had the pain tolerance of a cement post and was just as hard...in more ways than one. "You shouldn't have been doing that at all. It should have been *me* doing that. It should have been mine."

He caught her wrist, his warm hand closing around it

easily. The same hand that had been on his erection moments before. Her stomach tightened in response. "You were drunk, and if we fucked, you'd regret it in the morning. You're not just some girl in a bar, Lauren. I refuse to treat you like one for an orgasm. Is that so damn wrong?"

No. It wasn't wrong at all.

It was one of the things that made him such a good guy.

But her cheeks were red hot with embarrassment, and her stomach was twisting with desire, and screw being *reasonable*. She'd rather be naked and screaming his name. "I wasn't *that* drunk."

He snorted. "The hell you weren't. You're a damn lightweight. Let's not pretend otherwise. You were wasted off your ass, feeling horny, and you kissed me because I was the only guy there."

If only that was true. "It wasn't like that."

He snorted. "Funny. We've been friends for over twenty years, and you never acted like you thought about more than that until you pounded back some shots to prove a point."

"Neither have you, yet here you are. Masturbating on my couch while…what? Imagining me naked? Or were you fantasizing about someone else completely? Someone more your type than your lame little cupcake?"

His grip on her wrist tightened, and his gaze spit fire at her. "*Lauren*."

"*Steven*," she snarled back at him, breathing heavily. She yanked on her wrist, and this time he let her go. She backed up a step, toward her bedroom, rubbing her wrist. Not because it hurt. She could still feel him holding on to her, even though he wasn't. Finally, she said, "Let's just do what you said all along, and forget this ever happened. As far as I'm concerned, none of this *did* happen."

He curled his hands into fists at his sides. "The hell it didn't."

Oh my freaking God. The man made no sense. "You *just* told me a little while ago we had to pretend it never happened."

"That was before," he said, a muscle in his jaw ticking.

"Before what?" She wrung her hands in front of her. "You're obviously mad at me for kissing you, so I don't understand what your goal is here."

"I'm not mad at you for kissing me." He gritted his teeth together so hard it was a miracle they didn't crack. "I'm mad at how you did it."

She blinked at him. "What? That doesn't even make any—"

"That's not how our first kiss should have been. It's not the way it was supposed to go down. It should have—" He broke off and muttered a curse. "It should've gone like this."

And then she was in his arms.

His mouth was on hers, and his hands were everywhere, and all she could think was...*finally*. He swept her into his arms and carried her into her room, his mouth moving over hers without any hint of hesitation this time.

Earlier when he kissed her, it had been amazing.

She thought it couldn't get any better than that, and lost herself in the moment. To top it off, he'd made her come without even really having to try. But now that he was kissing her again, and he wasn't holding himself back from her, that kiss faded away into oblivion.

This, right here, was a *kiss*. And after he was finished with her, no other kiss in all of time would ever compare with his.

He dropped her onto the bed, covering his body with hers. "I'm not going to ask you again. Are you sure you want this?"

She nodded frantically, breathing fast and heavy. "Y-Yes. I'm sure."

"By the time I'm done, you're never going to forget what tonight felt like. What we did. For the rest of our lives, when we see each other, all we'll think about is this one night together. The only night I made you scream my name so loud it woke up the neighbors." He caught her hands above her head, holding them captive on her pillow. "And you're not allowed to hate me for it afterward."

She bit her lip. "I could never, *ever*, hate you."

Something flashed across his expression, and he twisted his lips. "I hope like hell you're right."

Then his mouth was on hers…

And she was a goner.

Chapter Seven

With Lauren's lips pressed against his, and her soft body underneath his, it was hard to remember why he fought against this in the first place. Hard to remember why this might very well be the worst mistake he ever made in his life. Or maybe, just maybe, it might be the best decision he ever made...

And he hadn't even *made* it yet.

No pressure, or anything.

He skimmed his fingers down the outside of her bare thigh and back up the inside. All night long, she stayed on his mind. He couldn't shut out the way she cried out his name as she came, her fingers digging into him as if she was never going to let go. And she hadn't. Even though he sent her to bed alone, she'd been with him the whole time.

In his head.

His raging erection hadn't let up over the past two hours, so he finally gave in and decided to take care of himself so he could get some damn sleep. All it had taken was him picturing her coming, with her back arched and her mouth parted, and he'd pretty much been there. Of course, the second he got close to orgasm, she popped in and caught him jerking off. And now nothing could help him but *her*.

Slowly, he inched his fingers toward her core, tracing her slit. She was wet and hot and ready, and he was so far gone he ached to slide into her warmth without wasting a damn second of their time together. But this was the *one* time he was letting himself have her, so it needed to be everything he'd dreamed of.

She needed to scream for mercy.

Hopping off the bed, he undid his pants and let them hit the floor. He kicked out of them and made quick work of removing the rest of his clothing. She watched from the bed, lifting up on her elbows and biting down on her swollen lower lip. There was obviously no need to hesitate at his nakedness. After years of friendship and that embarrassing moment on the couch, she'd seen it all now.

Once he was naked, he stood there, staring at her. "Too many clothes. Take them off slowly. I want to watch."

"Uh…okay." She let out a small laugh. "Seriously?"

He squared his jaw. If she wanted to fuck him, she'd get the real him. In bed, he didn't mess around. He ravished his partners, in every way, and left them trembling. But as he drove them insane with need, he always remained in control. Never forgot where he was, or what he was doing, or lost his head.

With Lauren, it was even more important he do exactly that. If he let himself slip, or remembered how much she meant to him, then he might put too much feeling into this. Into something that didn't need any feelings at all.

Sex was sex.

That's all this was.

He lifted a brow. "Do I look like I'm kidding around? I want to watch you undress, and then I'm going to worship your whole delicious body. Everywhere."

She swallowed hard, her tits rising and falling rapidly. "God."

"Nope. It'll be me in that bed, and it'll be my name you're calling out, not his, when I lick that sweet pussy of yours, and take you so hard you forget what it feels like not to have me buried inside of you." He raised a brow and crossed his arms. "Is that going to be a problem for you?"

A small groan escaped her. "N-No."

"Then undress. Now."

Sitting up, she licked her lips. "Steven."

"You're overthinking this too much. Just take it off."

Letting out a frustrated breath, she rose on her knees and gripped the bottom of her tank. She lifted it slowly, baring inches of skin at a time, but not nearly enough.

He held his breath. As much of *his* body as she'd seen, he hadn't seen anything on *hers* that wasn't normally covered by clothes. A bikini, at the least.

She could literally cut her clothes off of her with a pair of scissors, and it would still be the sexiest thing he'd ever seen. By the time the bottom swells of her tits peeked out, he clenched his fists and his breaths came out erratically. He'd never needed to see an article of clothing removed as much as he did right now. "Lauren."

She lowered it, hiding her breasts from him again. At first, it appeared to be a slip of the hand, but then she smirked and batted her lashes. "Yes…?"

"Take. It. Off."

She let it fall back into place, hiding all her delicious skin from him again, and cocked her head to the side. "Make me."

He growled, forgetting his command for her to strip, and all the reasons why he had to treat this like every other one-night stand he ever had. He was supposed to be in control of this whole affair, and yet he didn't feel in control.

At all.

She tried to scoot backward on the bed, away from him, but she was too slow. He easily caught up to her, grabbed her ankle, and yanked until she lay flat on her back. Her hair splayed across the bed, like some kind of brunette halo, and she watched him. His breath jammed in his throat. Her glowing blue eyes were filled with so much life, passion, need, and so much more he couldn't even begin to describe.

His fingers flexed on her ankle, and he swallowed hard. He couldn't do this. Couldn't forget where he was. Or that this was just another—oh the hell with it. This *wasn't* just another woman. It was Lauren. *His* Lauren. And there was no ignoring that.

Hell, he didn't want to ignore it.

Grabbing the waistband of her shorts, he tugged them down her thighs with one harsh pull. She gasped and grasped his bare biceps. "*Steven.*"

"Yep, still me."

Without looking at what presents he already bared, he yanked her shirt over her head, too, and finally…he *looked*. He'd waited so he could see the whole picture at the same time, with nothing in the way, and his patience was duly rewarded. After years of friendship, chaste hugs and kisses on cheeks, and clothes in the way…

It was his turn.

Her pale, smooth skin was flawless, and her tits were tipped with small, dusky rose nipples. Her waist was even smaller than he thought, even though he'd seen it millions of times before. Her hips flared out to ridiculously seductive proportions, and she had a light dusting of brown curls between her legs, but the rest of her was bare.

She was, in short, perfection.

Way too flawless for a guy like him.

"Lauren…" He ground his teeth together and brushed

her hair off her shoulder. He didn't want anything obstructing his view of her naked skin. "Shit."

She lifted up on her elbows, all soft lips and naked skin. "What's wrong?"

"Nothing." He skimmed his fingers over her skin, right under her tits. "I just need a second. You're beautiful."

Her cheeks flushed, and she lifted a leg, bending it at the knee, and her gaze dipped over Steven's body. It lingered on his abs. "You're not so bad yourself."

"Thanks, cupcake." His lips twitched into a smile, and he lowered his body on hers. The second their bare skin touched, he hissed, and she groaned. "Damn."

Nothing had ever felt as right as this.

Melding his lips to hers, he caught her hands and held them above her head as he ravaged her mouth. The time for words—and doubts—was over. She dug her heel into his ass, urging him closer. And then even closer.

It still wasn't enough. He needed to be inside of her.

Groaning, he deepened the kiss. She tasted like rum and a sweet flavor that was uniquely her, and he couldn't get enough. Her tongue sought and found his. This night, this time in her arms, would be unlike any other he'd ever had. Because she was *Lauren*.

His best friend.

Holding both her wrists captive with one hand, he traced the curves of her body, memorizing the way her soft, smooth skin felt under his rough fingertips. Everywhere he touched, goose bumps rose, and he slowly traced a path toward her left nipple. It puckered and hardened, begging for his touch, and who the hell was he to deny her?

He always gave her what she asked for.

Scraping the side of his thumbnail against it, he circled the hard bud. She whimpered into his mouth, arching her back and tugging on her arms. She was restless, and her need vibrated off of her, feeding his own. He broke off the kiss and nibbled a path down her neck, still not releasing her wrists.

"Steven," she breathed, her voice soft and pleading. "Please. Let me touch you."

He shook his head. "No."

"But—"

"I said *no*," he growled in reply, gripping her ass and hauling her against his hard dick roughly. "You feel that?"

She nodded frantically.

"One touch from you, and it'll be over. I want you too damn badly to let you touch me right now. So you'll wait till I tell you that you can, and that won't be until I worship your body completely. It won't be until you're quivering and sweating and crying from the pleasure I've already given you." He rolled his hips against her, pressing against her clit. "Understood?"

Again, she nodded frantically, her hands curling into fists.

"I'm going to let go of you now, so I can use both hands to fuck you properly, but if you touch me, if you move without my permission…I stop." He dug his fingers into the side of her ass possessively, and nipped at the side of her neck. "Got it?"

A small moan escaped her, but she nodded. "I'm going to get you back for this. One way or another, I will."

Doubtful, but he would allow her to keep her little revenge plan. "If you say so."

He let go. She didn't move.

Without wasting a second, he closed his palms over both her breasts, rolling her nipples between his thumbs and pointer fingers as he took her mouth again. She moaned and writhed beneath him, but she didn't move her hands. When he pinched her nipples, she curled her legs around his waist.

He should pull free, since he hadn't told her to do that, and he was in control. But…he didn't want to. She felt way too damn good, wrapped all around him. He pressed even closer to her, his bare dick teasing her core and his teeth digging into her lower lip, and she strained against him.

For some reason, he couldn't shake the feeling that he would never get close enough to her for satisfaction. And that was the craziest part of this whole thing. That all these years, this combustible passion had just been sitting there, waiting to be lit.

And he hadn't even seen it.

He slid down her body, licking her sweet, damp skin as he went. Her shoulder. Over her heart, which raced. He paused over her tits, unable to resist drawing a deep pink bud into his mouth. He sucked hard, slipping his hands between her legs as he did so.

The second he touched her clit, she cried out and lifted her hips, breathing heavily. When he thrust two fingers inside her wet heat, she screamed, "God. *Yes.*"

He stopped, his fingers still buried inside her. All he could hear was the steady, rushed thumping of his heartbeat. It demanded he stop playing games and take her, but he ignored it. "What did I tell you?"

She stiffened. "I didn't move my hands. I swear it."

"I know." He pressed a thumb to her clit, applying enough pressure to drive her higher up the crest, but not over it. "You said 'God.' He's not here, I am."

She made a frustrated sound and moved her hips restlessly. "*Steven.*"

"Say it again." He pulled his fingers out, hovering at her entrance. "Say it, and I'll let you come."

Her nostrils flared. "*Let* me come?"

"Yeah." He teased her clit with his thumb, tracing it lightly. "Hard. Fast."

"Oh my—*gah.*" She cut herself off in the nick of time. She looked like she was two seconds from killing him or fucking him. "Steven."

"My Steven." He buried his face in her neck and flicked his tongue over her racing pulse. "I like that."

He thrust his fingers deep inside her, rubbing her clit at the same time, and caught her mouth. She kissed him back frantically, her hips pumping up and down as he moved his fingers inside of her, mimicking what he would be doing to her in just a few minutes with his dick. When she cried out and tensed, burying her hands in his hair, Steven took his hand away, denying her the orgasm he promised her.

She screamed out in frustration and punched his arm. "I'm going to *kill*—"

Slowly, oh so slowly, he grasped her wrist and set her hand back above her head where he commanded she keep it. He watched the acknowledgment of what she did light her expression, and she moaned. "It was an accident. I swear. Please, I need—"

"I know what you need," he said, his voice low and his grip on her wrist unwavering. "You need me to fuck you with my mouth, and you need my dick inside of you. And you'll get it. You'll get all of it—if you follow my rules."

She nodded, biting down on her lip. "I will. I am."

"Good."

He kissed her again, lingering on her sweet lips because he just couldn't get enough, before slowly lowering himself over her body. He dropped kisses on her sweet skin again, not stopping at her breasts this time. He kept going till he knelt between her legs. She closed her thighs on either side of his head, holding him in place, and he ran his tongue up her slit, unable to resist getting a taste.

"Steven," she groaned, arching her back even higher. "Please."

He couldn't look away from her. Flushed cheeks. Parted lips. Hard pink nipples, pointing up and begging for more. It all tantalized him. And he couldn't wait any longer.

She had to scream his name again.

Lowering his head, he slid his hands under her ass, and lifted her up to his mouth. She smelled delicious. Like *Lauren*. Rolling his tongue over her clit, he scraped his teeth against the tender flesh before closing his mouth over her and sucking. She rolled her hips in a figure eight motion, her whole body quivering under his intimate kiss. He tightened his grip on her ass, digging his fingers in a little roughly, testing out the waters.

She pressed even closer to him, making his grip harsher. "*More.*"

Groaning, he deepened the strokes of his tongue. At the same time, he slapped the side of her ass, and she cried out, lifting her hips higher and moving more frantically. He rolled his tongue over her, losing track of how long he knelt there, at the doors of heaven, and he could have stayed there forever. He slapped the side of her ass again, and...

She *came*.

Her head fell back, and her hips writhed as they lowered to the mattress, and she let out a soft moan as she collapsed, lips parted and body lax. When she hit the mattress, she bit down on her lip and ran a hand over her hard nipple, dragging across it with a moan.

It was, hands down, the hottest thing he'd ever seen in his whole tainted life.

He didn't even care that she moved her hands. All the rules, and reasons, for why he fucked the way he did faded away, and he couldn't stop staring at that hard, pert nipple that clearly asked to be teased again.

"Do it again," he rasped. "Touch yourself."

She locked eyes with him, cheeks flushed...

And she did it.

Chapter Eight

There was no longer a single doubt in her mind that if Steven was *any* other man than her non-committal best friend…he could be the man she'd been waiting for her whole life. Everywhere he touched burned. Everything he didn't touch ached. Never in her whole life had she ever felt as alive as she did now…

And that was the real kicker.

She understood how men worked. Their thoughts, and their fears. Even better than that, she knew *his*. The second he came, he would already be searching for a way to forget this ever happened. To pretend he hadn't succumbed to her for a night of passionate lovemaking, and let himself go. And she couldn't—*wouldn't*—fool herself into thinking otherwise. This was a one-time thing, and it could never, ever happen again.

But that didn't mean she was willing to be forgotten.

To be another notch on his bedpost.

All those men she dated and ditched had been practice for this. And by the time she finished with him, Steven Thomas wouldn't have the foggiest notion of what hit him.

And he certainly wouldn't forget he'd had her.

Licking her lips, she ran her fingertips over her nipple again, watching *him* as he watched her. "Mmmm…"

He flexed his jaw, spellbound by the sight. He was all about control in bed, and she had a feeling that was all a ploy to make sure he didn't forget who she was, or that this was a temporary arrangement, but she wasn't going to let him get away with it.

They had history. Feelings. Years together.

"Like this?" she asked, dragging her nails over it and moaning. "Or harder?"

His jaw flexed, and he gripped her thighs roughly. "Harder."

"Yes, sir," she breathed, watching the effect of her words on him. "Do you like to be called sir?"

His nostrils flared, and he skimmed his fingers over her stomach, up her ribs, and under her breasts. The gentle touch was at war with the intensity of his expression and his tense jaw. He still focused on her hand, watching her touch herself. "It's a first for me, but I'll allow it."

She pulled on her nipple and closed both hands over her breasts, letting out a soft sigh. "Okay. Now what?"

His breathing quickened, and he rolled off the bed to his feet. Bending down, he opened the top drawer on her nightstand, pulled a condom out and tossed it next to her, before shutting it again. It didn't surprise her that he knew where to find them. He'd taken some from her before for impromptu one-night stands. That's the kind of friends they were. And now they were *naked* friends. *Oh, God.*

Walking back to the edge of the bed, he stood there, watching her, and grabbed his cock. He frowned. "I didn't tell you to stop playing with yourself, did I, Lauren?"

Seeing him hold himself like that, like he'd been doing earlier…

It stole her breath away. But she could tell, just by looking at him, that he'd regained that control he held so freaking dear, and he held it close to his chest this time. "What do you want me to do now, sir?"

"You'll find out soon enough," he said, teasing her with those featherlight touches on his cock. "Maybe I'll fuck you now? Or should I continue my teasing...?"

"Or I could have a turn," she said quickly, licking her lips and staring at his impressive erection. Ever since she found him on the couch, stroking it, she hadn't been able to stop thinking about giving him that kind of pleasure with her mouth. Rolling to her knees, she crawled across the king-size bed and knelt at the edge. Hesitantly, since he hadn't given her permission to do so, she ran her finger down his hard length, tracing that blue vein that had caught her eye earlier. "I still owe you that medal."

He swallowed so hard his Adam's apple bobbed. "You want that?"

"I do." She nodded. "So badly."

Burying his hands in her hair, he guided her closer. "You have two minutes. That's all you—" He broke off on a strangled moan. "*Fuck*."

She licked him from base to tip, not wasting a second of the time he allotted, before wrapping her lips around the head and sucking. She let out a soft moan.

He fisted her hair, his whole body held tightly. The muscles on his arms strained and flexed, and he pushed into her mouth a little more. She pressed her thighs together, needing him inside her so desperately it physically hurt.

"Lauren." He swallowed hard. "Christ, your mouth is so small and hot. You feel so good. So tight."

Hollowing out her cheeks, she took more of him in, sucking and licking and trying her best to drive him as crazy as he drove her. She cupped his balls and tugged, taking more of him in and increasing suction as she rode her mouth up and down his length.

Relaxing her throat, she took in his whole cock, and he let out a strangled moan. He pulled on her hair, tugging her back and forcing her to let go. The second he was out of her mouth, he shoved her back on the bed and kissed her as if he was dying and needed air, and the only way he would get it was through her.

And she felt the same exact way.

Locking her hands behind his neck, she kissed him back, moaning when he pressed his erection against her core. "Shit." With harsh motions, he grabbed the condom, ripped it open, and rolled it on. As soon as the protection was taken care of, he gripped her leg, hauled it up by his waist, and positioned himself between her thighs. "Hold on tight, cupcake."

And he kissed her, seizing her mouth as he slid inside her with one long, sure stroke. He didn't stop till he was all the way in, and when he was, he froze, his whole body tensing. It was almost as if he treasured the moment, letting it hit him, before he moved again. And once he moved…

He didn't stop.

His hands roamed all over her body, touching every square inch of her, and he kissed her as if he was never planning to stop, never breaking contact as he moved inside of her, filling her in a way she'd never been filled before. The whole time he made love to her, he drove her higher and higher over the crest, dragging her along whether she was ready to go or not.

But, God, she was.

When he curled his hand under her butt and lifted her higher, she gasped into his mouth. He hit a spot she only ever read about in books. Her scalp tingled, her fingers went numb, and blinding pleasure shot through her veins.

Pulling back, he groaned and buried his face in the crook of her neck, nipping the sensitive skin there. "Christ, Lauren.

You're so fucking tight, and wet, and you smell like heaven."
He slammed into her, hitting that spot again. "I need to hear
you scream my name."

He slid his hand between them, rubbing against her clit,
and drove inside of her. She bit down on her lip hard, trying
to hold it back, but he did it again, and whispered, "That pussy
is so damn hot. So damn *mine*. Stop fighting it, and give me
what I want."

This time, when he moved inside of her and teased her
clit, she did it. Her whole body tensed, stars flew in front of
her, and she came. "*Steven!*"

He growled possessively, gripping her thigh with his
free hand so tightly it would leave bruised fingermarks on
her skin as evidence of this night, and slammed into her,
his movements still timed and strong, but more erratic. His
breathing increased and grew more ragged with each stroke,
and watching him lose himself inside of her drove her
impossibly higher all over again.

His mouth caught hers, and she clung to him, letting him
take her on the crazy ride she would never forget. When he
stiffened over her, his breath whooshing out of him, she was
right there with him, coming even harder than the last time.
He collapsed on top of her, his arms on either side of her
head, and let out a few soft curses. "*Lauren.*"

She tried to gather her scattered thoughts, but they were
all over the place. There was no getting them back anytime
soon. "Yeah?"

"That was—" He pulled back and rested on his elbows.
He studied her face, still buried inside of her, and swallowed.
"Are you okay?"

"Okay?" She frowned. "Yeah. Of course I am. Why
wouldn't I be?"

"I kind of lost control at the end. Forgot who I—" He
glanced at her mouth, then slammed his attention back

northward. "I don't do that shit. Don't lose control of myself. I'm sorry."

Lauren fought back the smile trying to escape. "It was great. Everything was…amazing." Damn him, it had been.

It had all been *too* good.

"Do you still want me to stay?" He pulled out of her and rolled to his feet. "When you asked me here, you weren't planning on fucking me."

"It's fine." She sat up and hugged her knees, watching him as he headed for the bathroom. Every step he took was harsher than the last. She could see him analyzing everything already. Coming up with all the reasons why them sleeping together had been a bad idea. Taking the fun out of it. "I'm fine, and I still want you to stay."

He gave her a hard look, and shut the bathroom door behind him.

She dropped her forehead on her knees and sighed. He was making this weird when it didn't need to be. It was just sex. It didn't mean anything. They were still friends. And he was still her favorite person.

The water turned on, and off again.

A few moments later, he came out. He strode to the bed, rubbed the back of his neck, and opened his mouth to speak. Probably to make some excuse or another about why he shouldn't stay. "Lauren—"

"Am I allowed to move my arms yet?"

He choked on a laugh. "Uh—yeah."

"Good." She grinned. "'Cause I already did. Obviously."

He stared at her, still way too serious. "Lauren—"

"*Stop*." She shook her head at him. "It was just sex, Steven. Stop worrying about what comes next. I'll tell you what comes next. We go back to normal. So stop looking at me as if you broke me, and get over it."

"What?" He flushed. "I'm not."

"Yeah, you are. And it's annoying. I'm not some weak little girl who needs your protection." She kicked the covers to the bottom of the bed and got out of it. "Would you be acting like this with any other woman you just finished screwing?"

He crossed his arms and glowered at her—still gloriously naked. And she couldn't look away from the work of art he was. Black ink swirled all over his chest, and arms, and he had one tattoo right below his belly button. A red dragon. It was her favorite one. "I haven't even said anything yet. How do you know what I'm think—?"

"You don't need to say anything. I can see it all over your face." She stalked toward the bathroom, needing to get away from him for a few minutes. He was still looking at her as if she was a fragile thing that couldn't handle a night in his arms, and it was annoying. "Believe it or not, I've had sex before. I've even had one-night stands. I'm not going to cry or accuse you of sullying my good name, or suddenly think you're in love with me because you gave me some orgasms. And I'm definitely not about to fall at your feet like the rest of the girls you slept with, because you had me once—and now I *have* to have more. So knock it off, and stop being so serious."

He grabbed her arm as she passed. Despite her words, her heart immediately picked up speed, and her body came to attention. In spite of her words, she did want him again. And again. And *again*. She was just smart enough to admit it couldn't happen. They'd had their fun, now it was time to move on. "So you're going to be able to keep on going on as we have before, acting like I don't remember what kind of moan you make when you come?"

"Sure. Why not?" Her cheeks heated. "Can you think of a reason we can't do that?"

"One night." He tightened his grip on her. "That's what we agreed to."

"I know. I was there." She smiled, pulled free, and headed

toward the bathroom again. "So stop looking at me like I'm going to break. You're not *that* good, Steven."

Oh…but he was. He really, really was.

The jerk.

"Is that a challenge?" He rubbed his jaw. "I can't resist a challenge."

She forced a laugh and grabbed her robe off the bathroom door. After shrugging it on and pulling it shut so he could no longer see her boobs, she felt a bit more in control of the conversation. "Call it what you want. I call it fact. We had sex, it was fun, but now we can pretend it never happened, and go back to our regularly scheduled lives as best friends."

A muscle in his jaw ticked, right above where his fingers rested. "That easy?"

"That easy." She added a shrug for good measure. "We've slept in a bed together before. Let's treat it like that's all that happened."

His shrewd gaze was way too intent for her liking. And she was probably imagining it, but it was almost as if he was… *pissed*. When he caught her staring, he replaced the expression with a bland look and a smile. "All right," he said, stepping back and dropping his hands to his sides and scanning the floor. Bending over, he picked up his boxers. "Consider it done."

She swallowed hard as he stepped into his underwear, his muscles flexing and stretching and—*oh my God*, he caught her staring. Plastering a smile on, she nodded once. "Excellent. Glad it's settled. Now if you'll excuse me…?"

"Good night," he called out.

"Night!" She slammed the door shut behind her.

Leaning against it, she breathed heavily. The only thing she could think about was all the magical things he'd done to her with his tongue, and his hands, and his big hard— "Stop it," she whispered to herself.

Shaking her head, she washed up and walked back into

her room, but tripped over her own feet. Her bed wasn't empty. She stumbled forward, but caught herself before she hit the floor. "W-What are you doing?"

"Sleeping." He yawned, covering his mouth. "What's it look like I'm doing?"

"Lying in my bed," she pointed out, hugging herself.

"Like you said, we've slept together tons of times before, so if we want to go back to normal"—he shrugged and yawned again, but she didn't miss the challenge he issued to her, it was written all over his expression—"I figured we might as well sleep together again tonight. Get the awkward part over with right away. If what we did meant nothing to us, we wouldn't hesitate to sleep together, right? We wouldn't think it was weird. We'd just go on and have a fun sleepover."

Yeah. Fun. "Right. Of course. Good thinking."

Without another word, she climbed into the bed, rolled away from him, and yanked the covers over herself. He lay directly beside her on his back, his body heat emanating toward her like a freaking beacon or something, and let out a soft moan. Her heart picked up speed at the sound. It was undeniably sexy.

"Night, cupcake."

"Good night," she whispered back, staring blankly at the wall while trying to pretend she didn't even notice he was there.

"Oh, by the way?" He rolled toward her and ran his fingers over her cheek from behind her, his touch gentle and almost nonexistent. "That's how I would have done it."

She swallowed, not saying anything.

Quite frankly, she had nothing to say to that in the first place. Steven's breathing evened way too fast, like usual, and soon he was asleep. She lay there a little while longer, trying to shut him out of her mind. It didn't work. Every time she closed her eyes…

He was *there.*

Chapter Nine

The next morning, Steven woke up before Lauren, even though he hadn't slept more than an hour or so, after she basically told him that last night meant *nothing* to her. From any other woman, this would be great news. The last thing he needed was his one-night stands falling in love with him.

But she wasn't just a fling.

The fact that she could fuck him and forget him like he meant nothing—well, it kinda pissed him the hell off. No matter how much he denied it, or how many times he acknowledged how wrong he was for her, all he could think about was what she did to him with that damn tongue of hers…

And when they could do it again.

For the first time in his adult life, he woke up craving more from a woman. There was no denying that his usual wham, bam, thank you ma'am wasn't enough with Lauren. This was an entirely new feeling for him. One he couldn't handle, quite frankly.

Sleeping in bed with her had been impulsive. There had been booze, and kisses, soft touches, long repressed desires let loose. But he hadn't *planned* it.

And now he had no damn clue what to do.

Rolling out of bed, he stretched and yawned, glancing over his shoulder at the clock. It was seven thirty, and he didn't have to work today. Neither did she.

So why the hell was he so damn awake?

He turned back to Lauren, frowning. She slept peacefully, her back to him, and she hadn't moved all night. He'd pretended to fall asleep, giving him a chance to think in some peace and quiet. He'd lain awake throughout most of the night after they...what? Made love? Fucked? What should he even call last night? It had been different than any other experience he ever had. And he couldn't stop thinking about it — or her. Or how she made him feel. What they could be, if only he dared to find out.

And if he forgot all the reasons she deserved better.

As if she could sense his thoughts, her brow wrinkled and she squirmed, letting out a soft sigh. She mumbled something under her breath, squirmed some more, and rolled over, reaching across the bed as if she sought him out. He waited to see if she would wake up, but she settled back in and breathed evenly once more.

Over the span of his adult life, he faced bombs, bullets, war, and death. He could kill another man without blinking an eye, if it was for a good cause. He could shoot, bomb, fight, fuck, and drink. But when it came to *living*, to taking a chance on something like him and Lauren, he hesitated. When it came time to try maybe *being* happy...

He wasn't sure he could do it.

If that wasn't dysfunctional, he didn't have a clue what was.

Crawling back into the bed carefully, he lay completely still, staring at her nightstand, while trying not to freak the hell out about all the "feelings" shit going through his head.

What he'd seen inside of it, through the glass lid, had triggered a memory…

One long forgotten.

It was nine years ago, when he'd just gotten back from his first tour overseas, and he and Lauren were alone—just the way he liked it. They hiked to their favorite pond in the woods, because he told her he needed some peace and quiet.

She instantly helped him get it.

After a few drinks and a couple of hours, she rested her head on his shoulder, sighing contentedly. Even now, he could still remember the way the sunlight hit her hair, and the way her blue eyes sparkled, like it was yesterday…

Reaching out, he smoothed her soft hair out of her face. She watched him closely, biting down on her lower lip. "What was it like over there?"

"Awful. Bloody. Hot." Steven shrugged and turned away, not wanting her to see him. He lifted the beer to his lips and took a swig, but it tasted bitter. "I don't know how people do stuff like we do over there, and come home to their wives and kids. How they just…go back to normal."

"Do you wish you had a wife to go home to?" she asked, still staring at him as if she read his thoughts and knew him better than he did. Sometimes, he thought she just might. "Or kids?"

"I don't need a wife. I have you." He scooted closer and threw his arm over her shoulder. She rested her head on his chest again, snuggling in. He immediately felt at peace with the world. He had her in his arms. "That's much better."

"What if that changes, though?" She tilted her face up to his. Her mouth was inches from his. His heart rate increased, though he didn't understand why. "Even worse, what if neither of us gets married? Like, ever?"

He snorted. "Why would that be bad?"

"We'd be alone." She sighed. "That's sad."

"We wouldn't be alone, we'd be together." He laughed, gripping his beer bottle tighter. "Hell, if we're still single at thirty, we might as well get married."

She chuckled. "Yeah, sure. Whatever."

"I'm serious," he said, sitting up straight. Reaching behind him, he grabbed the yellow twist tie off the bread they'd brought for sandwiches. He made quick work of turning it into a ring shape, holding it out to her with a silly grin. "Lauren Brixton, if you're single when I'm thirty, will you marry me out of pity?"

She stared at him, all wide blue eyes and soft pink lips. After a long, pregnant pause, she extended her left hand. It trembled. "Yes. It would be an honor."

Well, he'd turned thirty a little over three weeks ago…

And they were both single. Fuuuuccccckkkkkk.

She rolled over again, her lids drifting up. For a second, she smiled and stretched. When she reached over and felt skin…she froze, the smile slipping away. Slowly, she turned her head toward him. Her eyes were the same bright blue they'd been that day at the pond. Her nose was still small and pert, and she still had freckles across her cheeks. But she was older. Wiser. More beautiful.

And she looked as if she would rather be anywhere but here.

With him.

"Hey," he said, giving her a small smile, when he really would rather pull her in his arms and kiss her again. "Morning, sleepyhead."

"Morning," she squeaked, pulling the covers up to her chin and hanging on to them with a death grip. "You're up early."

"Yeah. I woke up when a truck beeped outside, and I couldn't fall back asleep. So, I just waited for you to wake up." He paused. "Which you did. Now."

She blinked at him.

He smiled back at her.

Swallowing hard, she cleared her throat. "So, uh…"

Cocking a brow, he asked, "Yes?"

"This is so weird," she finally said in a rush, laughing and scooting into a sitting position. She dragged the sheet with her. "Which is stupid, right? I mean, it was *sex*. We've both done it before. Just not…with each other. You know?"

She was clearly nervous.

"I'm pretty sure I'd remember all the things I did to you last night," he agreed. "So, yeah, I do."

Her cheeks pinked. "I'd hope so."

"Oh, I would," he said, dipping his voice down low. "The things I did to you, cupcake, aren't something I'll forget."

She stared at him, not blinking, mouth ajar.

He grinned.

Another nervous laugh escaped her. "Yeah…so now we go back to normal, right?"

"Right." Reaching out, he tugged on a piece of her hair, still smiling. "It's not like we're dying to rip each other's clothes off again, or like you're gonna fall at my feet begging for more. I wasn't *that* good."

She swallowed hard, her cheeks going pink. He turned her own words back on her, and then laughed. "Uh…right. No offense."

"None taken. That would be foolish," he said, tugging harder. "Even if it would feel really, really good. The things you do with that tongue—damn, cupcake. That was like artwork. I'm not gonna lie, I wouldn't mind feeling that again, despite it all."

A small moan escaped her, but she killed it off quickly, her cheeks going even pinker. But he'd *heard* it. "Perhaps it's best not to talk about that kind of stuff?"

"Oh." He let go of her hair and stood, stretching his arms high above his head, smiling innocently. She watched him, her breaths quickening and her nostrils flaring, desire clear in her eyes. "Yeah, you're probably right. And I probably shouldn't mention how much you liked it when I licked your—"

"*Steven.*"

He laughed. "Right, right. Sorry." He wasn't. "So sorry." Still wasn't.

She scooted out of bed and tucked her hair behind her ears. "You have to work today, right? And I have to go into the bakery and—"

"It's Sunday," he reminded her. "We're off."

"You might be, but I'm not." She let out a short, musical laugh. "I have to go in and make a cake. It's getting picked up at four."

He cocked a brow. "You didn't mention this to me last night."

She glanced at him quickly. "Last night, we weren't exactly *talking*, were we?"

"That's not true," he said, picking up his pants. "I did a lot of talking."

There she went again with the blushing. "Oh my—" She cut herself off, throwing a quick glance his way. "I mean, yeah. I guess you did."

He knew exactly that she was thinking about. He was, too.

They were both thinking about last night, and the things they did to each other, and that made his dick harden and his gut tighten. It took all of his control not to grab her and kiss her. It would be so easy to remind her what exactly it was she was trying so damn hard to forget. "What can I say? I'm a talker," he said, shrugging.

"I noticed," she said drily. "I was there, too."

He grinned. "I also noticed."

A small laugh escaped her. "Okay, well, I'm going to shower and head into the bakery." She walked backward toward the bathroom, her gaze still locked on his. "You can hang out here, if you want, and wait for me to get—"

"Nah." He buttoned his pants. "I'll go back to my place, grab some clothes for the next few days, then meet you at your shop so I can help you out. It'll go quicker that way, and when we're finished, we can go together to meet up with everyone for drinks at five."

She froze, half bent over, pert little ass in the air, and dropped the shirt she'd pulled out of her drawer. Turning slowly, she eyed Steven like he was this unrecognizable thing. "You want to *bake* with me? In my shop? All day long?"

"Yeah," he said, pulling the zipper up. "Sure. Why not?"

"You've never asked to go to work with me before." She stood up straight. "You don't like baking. And you don't like how hot the kitchen gets when the oven is on. So why now?"

Last night she'd made him travel through space and time with her mouth and her soft touches, and he'd be damned if he was going to walk away after that.

"Why not?" he asked, shrugging into his dress shirt from last night. He didn't bother to button it. "Besides, you said you didn't want to be alone, right?"

"I did say that, didn't I?" she muttered, blowing her hair out of her face with a breath. "All right. Hey, I might have some clothes here, if you don't feel like going home on a walk of shame."

He frowned. "I left clothes here? When?"

"No, they're from Max—the guy before Brian. With the beard." She quirked her lips. "He was about your size, and he never came back to get them after we broke up."

Wear her ex's clothes? Yeah, he would rather walk down the street in a pink fucking tutu. He scowled at her, gripping his bow tie with his left hand, while he mentally imagined strangling Max with it. He'd hated that prick even more than he'd hated Brian. "Hell no. I'm not wearing his shit."

"Okaaaaay," she said slowly, eyeing him weirdly. "Suit

yourself."

He forced a tight smile, trying to hide his irritation. "I'll just run home, change, and meet up with you at the bakery. Deal?"

"Deal," she said, picking her gray shirt up again.

As he walked past her, he stopped by her side, hesitating.

He almost leaned in and kissed her, but nothing had changed between yesterday and today, so he settled for a shoulder squeeze. "See ya soon, cupcake."

"Yep," she said, her voice soft. "Bye."

He grabbed the rest of his shit, stepped into his dress shoes, and went out the door. The second he rounded the corner, and started down his own street—he lived three blocks away from her, because they planned it that way—he pulled his almost dead phone out of his pocket and dialed number two on his speed dial.

It rang three times, then, "Hello?"

"Holt, I'm going to fucking kill you," he growled.

A shuffling sound. "What did I do this time?"

"You were right." Steven glared up at the sunny sky. "That's what you did."

"I usually am, but you'll have to be more specific." Holt cleared his throat. "I was right about…?"

Steven gritted his teeth and waited to cross the road, saying the one word that would tell his buddy everything he needed to comprehend the situation at hand. "*Lauren.*"

Chapter Ten

Lauren paced back and forth, nibbling on her thumbnail until there wasn't much of it left to chew on. When a knock sounded on the front door, she sprinted to it, peeking out before opening it all the way. After her Brian "scare" last night…she was still a little on edge. "Oh, thank God you're here."

Her friend Daisy blinked at her. She held two to-go cups of coffee, and appeared to be still half asleep. Her red hair stuck up in the back, as if she'd forgotten to brush it, and she had bags under her eyes. But she was there, and that's all that mattered. "What's so important that you called me at eight o'clock with an SOS message on a Sunday morning to—"

"I slept with Steven," Lauren blurted out, stepping back so Daisy could come in. "And it was incredible. Life changing. Earth shattering."

Daisy gasped and came in, kicking the door shut behind her. "Oh, holy crap. That's totally SOS worthy. Tell me everything. And don't you dare leave out a single detail."

Lauren flopped back on the couch—in the same spot

that Steven had been sitting in last night when she found him jerking off. That *did* things to her. Things she had no right feeling since last night had been a one-time thing, and it was just for *fun*, and God, she was so sick of that word. "I will, but the bad stuff first. I kind of sort of lied to him."

"Oh, crap." Daisy sat beside her, tucking her foot underneath and turning toward Lauren. Holding the coffee mug out, she pursed her lips and blinked those bright green eyes at her. "He hates liars."

"Yeah," she groaned.

Steven and Daisy didn't hang out. They didn't run in the same circles. But since Daisy was one of Lauren's only friends that wasn't also friends with *Steven*...she knew everything about him. And Lauren's attraction to him that she tried so hard to deny and ignore. Or, she had up until last night, anyway, when she ignored it all in the name of *fun*.

"Why would you do that?"

"I didn't really have a choice." Lauren shook her head, staring down at the coffee mug. "Okay, that's a lie. You always have a choice. But I was worried about him. He's been drinking a lot, and both Lydia and Holt asked me to help keep an eye on him."

Daisy whistled through her teeth and reared back. "Wait, so you *slept* with him to keep him *around*?"

"What? No. God, no."

"I don't get it." Daisy sipped her cappuccino. "How did you lie to him, then?"

She sipped her coffee, too, and it scalded her tongue. "Brian snuck in when I was in the shower, and I didn't know it was him. When I heard footsteps, I called Steven and he, of course, came running. By the time I realized it was just Brian coming to get his stuff, Steven was here, and he looked so worried...and it occurred to me that the best way to keep him here was to ask him to stay because I was scared. I was right.

It worked."

"Wow. So the sleeping together part just kinda happened?"

Lauren blew out a breath. "Yeah. I decided he needed to be reminded how fun life was, and then he was there, staring at me…"

The way his eyes had heated as he stared at her, as if he was thinking about kissing her, would forever be burned in her memory. No matter how many years passed, last night would go down in history as the most amazing night ever. And if she wished she could have more nights like that?

Oh well.

He didn't. And they wouldn't.

After watching men walk away from her for most of her life, she learned not to get attached to anyone, or anything. She didn't really lose sleep when they left her life. You'd have to care about someone to, you know, miss them. But Steven didn't fall into that category. Never Steven.

If she lost him…

God. She couldn't. It wasn't an option. Which was why it was so important to pretend she didn't want, or need, more. So she didn't scare him off.

"Earth to Lauren." Daisy snapped her fingers. "Hello? Anybody home?"

Lauren jerked back into the present. "Sorry. So sorry. Uh…what were you saying again?"

"What happened after you kissed him? Did he freak out?"

Lauren frowned. "Yeah. He pushed me away and sent me to bed alone after he…well. Got me there."

Her cheeks got hot. Despite all the men she dated and lost, she didn't really sleep with a lot of them. And when she did, she didn't *tell* everyone about it.

Or give a play by play.

Daisy flipped her bright red hair over her shoulder. "Do

go on."

"I'm not good at this," Lauren muttered. "Plus, this was different. It was intimate. Real. And when I kissed him, he took me there, and it was amazing, but he sent me to bed without actually, you know, having sex with me. And he didn't come."

"Wait. Hold up. I'm confused." Daisy held up a hand and frowned. "You said you *slept* with Steven."

"Yeah…"

"But you just said he got you off, and sent you to bed alone." Daisy cocked her head. "Which is it?"

Lauren fidgeted with the lid of the coffee, not sure how much she should say. To talk about what she and Steven had shared felt…wrong.

He was more than a story.

"After I went to bed, I came out to get some water. He was still awake and…watching TV. That's when we slept together."

Daisy blinked at her. "You're leaving out something."

"Lots of things," Lauren agreed. "But like I said, with Steven it was different. I don't want to tell you all the things we did. It's private."

"Oh my God," Daisy said, leaning back against the blue couch pillow. "You *suck*. Throw a girl a bone, man."

Lauren laughed. "I can't."

"Fine. Tell me this, though." Daisy pointed at her. "Do you want it to happen again?"

"It doesn't matter if I do or don't. It won't happen again. en made it very clear it was a one-night thing, and even if ln't, I'd know. It's what he does."

ut what if he's looking for something different from aisy asked, her voice quiet.

en turned away so her friend wouldn't see the opeful look that was probably on her face. "His feelings for me haven't changed at all after what we did. Neither have mine."

"That doesn't mean much at all," Daisy muttered.

"What?"

"Nothing," she said quickly, smiling.

"It's true," Lauren said defensively. "I feel the same."

"I don't doubt that. I just don't think you truly examined those feelings, or what they mean. And neither has he. He's a dude." Daisy sighed. "So what now? You pretend you didn't see how big his dick is and smile as he brings home woman after woman, all the while pretending like it doesn't hurt you when it does?"

Lauren choked on her coffee. When she could breathe again, she glowered at Daisy. "Pretty much."

"That's not going to happen," Daisy said, her tone speculative and her forehead wrinkled.

"Why not? We're adults. It happened, it was fun." Lauren lifted a shoulder. "And now it won't happen again. We go back to being platonic friends. Easy peasy."

Daisy snorted. "You, my dear, are crazy. No one does that."

"We will." Lauren lifted her chin. "I refuse to lose him. We screwed for one night. No big deal. I know him, and he's not looking to make this into something more. That's not his style. And I won't try to make it be. I won't try to change him."

Even if she wished, deep down, that for her he *would* change. That he'd think she was worth a real try at a relationship, even though in the end...

It would probably fail.

"But what if he *did*?" Daisy asked quietly, echoing her thought with crystal clear precision that was almost scary.

Lauren hesitated. The idea of trying for something real with him was...terrifying. Not because he would break her heart—which he very well might—but the idea of losing him was not something she was willing to consider.

Lots of friends had fleeting sexual relationships.

Not many exes remained friends.

"I have no idea," she answered honestly. "But luckily we were very honest with each other, and I'm okay with just the one time. So is he."

"Yeah, we'll see about that," Daisy muttered.

No. They wouldn't. And for some reason, that made her heart ache. "Enough about me," Lauren said, waving a hand. "Didn't you have a date last night?"

"No. My mom set me *up* on a date last night. I didn't go."

Lauren frowned, her heartache forgotten for Daisy's. "Why not?"

"You know why not." Daisy frowned. "Stop trying to take this off of you and Steven and the possibility of you two being a real couple. It's not going to work."

Lauren rolled her eyes like the mere idea was ludicrous. But, really, was it? Despite her words, and her worries, the idea of him wanting to *be* with her? To, like, love her and hold her close for the rest of his life? It made her heart race, and her knees shake, and her mind whirl, and her palms sweat, and…it didn't feel so crazy after all.

Scary, sure.

But not *crazy*.

"And that's what pissed me off the most, I think." Steven paced back and forth in front of Holt, who wore *Doctor Who* sweats, his glasses, and an inside-out black T-shirt. "She's all 'that was fun, let's go back to how things were,' and all I can think about is doing it again. Even though I shouldn't."

Holt sat on his couch, watching Steven carefully, and

rubbed his chin. He hadn't moved from his position at all, and Steven felt like he was in some kind of parallel universe where nothing made sense at all, and everything was fucked up. A steaming cup of coffee sat in front of him, half empty. Steven's was untouched. Lydia was still asleep in their bedroom. "Why not? And what, exactly, happened?"

"Dude." Steven stopped in front of him and crossed his arms. He still wore his clothes from last night. "What the fuck do you think happened? We braided each other's hair and talked about our dreams and desires while bonding over ice cream?"

Holt snorted, took his glasses off, and rubbed the bridge of his nose. "Yeah, but how far did it go? Kissing? Groping? Fucking?"

"We—had sex." Steven resumed pacing, biting back anything else he might say. He refused to call it *fucking*. It had been more than that. But it wasn't *lovemaking*, either. "And afterward, she immediately told me to stop looking at her as if anything changed, that we were the same as we were, and I needed to accept that. Like she already filed me in the past and moved on the second I let go of her. Which, normally I like, but with her, I didn't. I'm not sure why."

"I've got a few ideas," Holt said. His forehead wrinkled up and he pushed his glasses back into place. "So she wants it to be a one-time thing."

"Apparently." Steven picked up his coffee and took a big sip. "She was quite clear about that."

Holt blinked. "And you...*don't*?"

The shock in his friend's voice was not lost on Steven. He couldn't believe it, either. "No." He rubbed his face and let out a long breath. "But that doesn't change a damn thing. I can't be with her."

"Why not?" Holt asked, watching him with shrewd blue eyes. "You're single. She's single. What's holding you back?"

Steven refused to admit the real reason—that he wasn't good enough for a girl like Lauren. He had nightmares. Hated crowds. He never stopped looking over his shoulder for the next attack, even though he'd been out of the war zone for over a year now, and probably never would. And even now, to this day, he felt like a piece of him had died over there in that desert with the rest of his platoon.

The piece that deserved to be *happy*.

"I'm me, and she's her," he said, his jaw tight. "That's all the reason I need."

"I don't understand."

Steven rolled his eyes. "Have you met me? I don't do relationships. And the one time I did—"

"She cheated on you, and then broke up with you because you didn't 'love' her," Holt said drily. "I was there, too. It was a *year* ago."

It was true. He hadn't loved her. And he was pretty damn certain that the part of him that was capable of that emotion had been the part he'd lost overseas, sometime between his tenth kill and his last. In a warzone, after so many losses and deaths, you became immune to emotion.

Or, at least, he had.

"And she was right," Steven said, ignoring the sarcasm in Holt's comment. He set the mug down again, and paced. "I don't think I'll ever love a woman the way they want to be loved, and I refuse to do that to Lauren. She deserves more."

So damn much more.

"So maybe you could *be* more?" Holt said, shrugging. "Ever thought of that?"

Steven stared at him, completely taken aback.

He hadn't even really entertained the notion that he could change. That he didn't have to be the guy who didn't get the girl anymore. Rubbing his face with both hands, he explored his options. There was the obvious one. He could continue on as he'd been, pretending he didn't crave her as much as a drug addict did his next hit. Keep his distance and his soul intact... or as intact as it could be, anyway.

It's what he did best, after all.

Keeping a distance.

Or he could man up and fight for her, even though he wasn't sure what exactly it was that he fought for. He wasn't looking for an actual relationship with her...*was he*? Sure, it's what she deserved. But could he do that?

He wasn't so sure.

The one time he tried to fit into a box, and be a real boyfriend with Rachel, had been a disaster. He'd been a shitty boyfriend to Rachel, and he'd probably be an even shittier one to Lauren.

If he screwed everything up, he could lose her. That was what scared him, more so than the idea of him doing nothing did. Losing her would *kill* him.

He already accepted he wasn't good enough for her, and never would be. But he could try to be better. To do better. For her. All she had to do was ask...

And he'd give it 100 percent.

Maybe Lauren was the woman he had been waiting for his whole life, and he'd been too dumb to see it. Was he willing to continue being a dumbass, and risk losing her? Could he stand aside and watch her find another man who wasn't scared to let her into his heart? Watch her kiss him? Sleep with him? *Marry* him? Have his babies?

Fuck no.

The mere idea made him want to brutally murder a fictional man, so he got his answer. Now what was he going to do about it? All Steven did anymore was work, drink, and get laid. What kind of man would he be if he went from that, to being in a committed relationship with the best woman on Earth?

A bad one.

And he'd already done enough bad things.

If he was serious about being with her—if he was even *thinking* of entertaining the *possibility*—he needed to clean up his act first. Stop fucking. Stop drinking. Get his shit together. Then, and only then, would he have any right to get the girl.

And if he did all that and succeeded?

He'd fight like hell to keep her.

Chapter Eleven

If Lauren wasn't seeing it with her own two eyes, she would never believe it. Steven Thomas, the man who had no clue what an oven was for as far as she was aware, was *here*. Helping her bake a cake. With a smile on his face.

Whistling "The Star-Spangled Banner" under his breath.

She also couldn't believe he kept looking at her out of the corner of his eye, and quickly glancing away whenever she stared at him directly, as if he didn't want her to see — and *actually* thought he got away with it. She just couldn't figure out why he kept looking at her like she might bite.

The only thing she could guess was that he was trying to act as if they were fine, just like she was, and struggling. Did he regret last night? She didn't. Despite the fact that she had a feeling no other man would ever live up to Steven as a lover, one night in his arms was worth any lingering desire she still felt for him. A desire that she had a feeling would never fully go away. But whatever. She'd deal.

She was a big girl.

"What next?" he asked, brushing his wrist across his face

and leaving an adorable flour trail behind. His cheeks were flushed and he had bags under his eyes, but...he looked more alive than he had in weeks. Months, even.

Apparently, baking suited him.

She bit back a smile. "You're not finished stirring. You still have one more minute to go."

"Jesus," he muttered, glowering down at the bowl. "It's a miracle you don't have arms the size of The Rock's by now."

"Maybe I do," she teased.

He snorted and picked up the spoon again. He'd argued against hand stirring, wanting to use the mixer instead, until she told him it made for a smoother, richer cake—and that's what made her customers come back. Superior product. "Even if I hadn't just seen you naked, I would know for a fact that you don't."

"God," she muttered. "You just can't resist mentioning that again and again and again—"

"And again." He shot her a narrow-eyed glance that sent her pulse skyrocketing into dangerous territory. "Nope. I can't. If you saw you last night, you'd get it."

Damn him. He was good. Too good. And that irritated her. He shouldn't be so suave with her. "It's nothing you haven't seen a million times before."

"Trust me when I say it is," he said, his arms flexing with each sweep of the bowl he took. "It really fucking is."

She flushed. Like, *everywhere.* "You're not so bad yourself, you know."

And, of course, saying that reminded her of last night...

He continued stirring, not turning her way. "You're wrong there."

"Steven—"

"Don't. I'm an asshole and undeserving of someone like you." He set the spoon down with a *clank*, but the fake smile never slipped from his face. "Which, quite frankly, only made me want you more last night. I'm a selfish prick like that. Again, something we're both already aware of."

"I..." She shook her head. This perception he had of himself was so skewed and completely backward. "I have no idea why you think you're this horrible guy. What did you do when you were overseas that makes you think you're a monster?"

He flexed his jaw and picked the spoon back up. He stirred again, his motions faster and harder. "More shit than you would ever want to hear about."

"What makes you so sure?" she asked, shoving her bangs out of her eyes. "You never gave me a chance to decide that for myself, after all."

"I don't need to, damn it," he said, his easy, devil-may-care attitude slipping for the first time. "And who the hell said the bad things stopped when I came home? You yourself pointed out how much of a selfish asshole I've been, wasting away with booze and women. Do you think those women I fucked and forgot think I'm a *good* guy? Do *you* think I am, after last night?"

She didn't hesitate. "Yes. I initiated what happened last night. I wasn't some victim you have to make penance for, so stop trying to make me out to be one."

"Shit." He gripped the spoon tighter, breathing heavily. "You have no idea how hard it is for me to remember exactly why a guy like me shouldn't be with a girl like you."

"Wait, what?" Her heart traitorously picked up speed. "Do you...do you *want* to be with me again?"

He stared at her, his jaw flexing. "Do I ever?"

"No." She swallowed, cursing herself for even *thinking* he might be saying that. Way to make herself look like a fool. Plastering on a smile, she added, "But that doesn't make you a bad guy. It just makes you one who doesn't want a relationship. Not everyone does."

Slowly, oh so slowly, he turned her way. His hazel gaze blazed with...*need*? No, that couldn't be right. Not after what he just said. So why was he looking at her like that?

Uncomfortable with the silence, she blurted out, "You can stop stirring now. It's done. Uh, good job."

He set the spoon down beside the bowl. When he turned her way again, any sign of desire was gone. "What do you want me to do next?" he asked, his voice low.

Take me, right here, on the counter.

Running his hand through his hair, he leaned on the counter. He was so sexy, standing there, all hard muscles and bedroom eyes. He wore a tight-fitting blue T-shirt and a pair of ripped jeans that hugged him in all the right places. The cross tattoo on his arm stretched and moved as he moved his fingers through his thick hair.

And even though he stood there, not even making a move toward her, it felt like he was seducing. She licked her lips. "Uh..."

"It's not a trick question." He smirked, which should have annoyed her, but didn't. "I stirred it, so now I—?"

"Grease the pan, covering the whole bottom," she blurted out. "That's what you do. And make sure you do it thoroughly."

"Okay," he said, the smirk widening. "I'm nothing if not thorough when it comes to getting stuff nice and lubricated."

Yeah. She learned that up close and personal last night, thank you very much. "Uh...yeah. Great."

Picking up the pan, he wiggled it under her nose. His all too familiar cologne teased her senses, which didn't help her much when it came to resisting the urges he brought out in her. Especially after last night. "This one?"

She nodded and checked the temperature.

Since she didn't have anything to say, she said nothing at all. He approached, stopping directly behind her. He stood a respectable distance from her, no different than he would have done on any other occasion, but since she bent over to check the oven, it was…

Too *close*.

He was too close.

"Done."

"Now we put it in and bake it." She walked to the counter and made quick work of filling the pan. The whole time, he watched her in silence. By the time she was finished and put it in the oven, she was on edge and a little bit uneasy. She set the timer and turned around, dusting her hands off, and smiled even though the forced cheerfulness hurt her cheeks. "Okay. Now I'll—"

Turned out, facing him was a huge mistake. He was so close she had to step back to look up at him. But there was nowhere to go, so her butt hit the handle of the oven. She stumbled a little, resting her hands on his chest, and he gripped her biceps to help steady her. "Oops. Sorry. So sorry."

"It's fine." The second he grabbed her, all secure and tight, her stomach tightened and her breath quickened, so she instinctively reared away. He frowned. "Are you scared to touch me now?"

"N-No." Her cheeks heated. "Of course not. We're fine. I'm fine. Are you fine?"

"Of course," he said, running his thumbs over her skin, and his deep hazel eyes pulled her under his spell. "Why wouldn't I be?"

"I don't know," she answered. "Why wouldn't *I* be?"

He searched her face for something. Something she wasn't sure he would find. "You're acting weird. Like you're scared to be near me, or of me, even."

"I'm not," she answered defensively. He kept running his thumbs over her arm. It was distracting. And intoxicating. "I don't feel any differently toward you than I did last night, and that's the God's honest truth."

He tightened his hold on her. For some reason, her answer seemed to anger him. Well, if he expected her to beg him for more, he would be sadly disappointed. She wasn't that girl. "Bullshit."

"No. Not bullshit."

"Prove it," he dared her, his tone low and somehow seductive. "Prove you don't want me to kiss you, right here, right now."

Her heart sped up, and her mouth dried out. She swallowed uncomfortably. "And how, exactly, do you expect me to do *that*?"

"By kissing me." He splayed a hand across her lower back, possessive and commanding, and hauled her closer. She didn't even bother to resist. "Look the beast in the eye and show me it doesn't scare you."

She licked her lips, both hands still on his chest. "What good would that do? If I'm scared of kissing you, like you seem to think I am, what will doing it prove?"

"Asks the girl who locked herself in a closet because she was scared of dark, small spaces..." He dipped his hand lower, resting on the curve of her butt. "Just to prove she wouldn't let it get the best of her."

"I was fifteen and stupid," she said, cheeks flushed. "And you're comparing yourself to a closet."

"I'm all right with that." He lifted a shoulder. "Are you afraid it'll change your feelings for me?"

"No. Of course not." She tilted her chin up, staring up into those intoxicating hazel eyes. The challenge in his was impossible to ignore. "I could make out with you right here, and again—nothing would change between us."

He lowered his face to hers, stopping short of kissing her. "So. Kiss me."

All day long, she'd been trying to excuse last night as some sort of thoughtless, drunken decision that would never be repeated. But they were both dead sober now, and last night hadn't been a drunken night of impulsiveness. The truth was, in the years leading up to last night, she'd thought about the two of them a lot.

There had been tons and tons of warning thoughts.

She just chose to ignore them all and live in the moment last night. To take a chance. But now he was here, holding her, and asking her to do it again.

And, God help her, she was debating it.

Curling her hands into balls, she fisted his shirt and tugged him closer.

His gaze heated even more at the small movement, and his chest rose and fell rapidly. "Even though I shouldn't, I'm gonna tell you the truth. I lied earlier, when you asked me if I was thinking about having you again." His gaze roamed over her, heating her in places she'd never been heated before. "I've been thinking about it. All day. But the thing is, I've been trying not to."

She gripped his shirt so tightly her fingers ached. "Me, too."

"All I can think about is making you scream my name again. And I want to hear that sexy little moan you let out when you come. It can't possibly be as hot as I remember it being. I want to make you come, again and again, until the urge is dead, and I can go back to not wanting to rip your clothes off every time I see you," he said, his hand slipping down to cup her butt and pull her impossibly closer. "But if you don't feel the same way, say the word. I'll never mention how fucking hot you look when you come, or how badly I want to bury my dick inside of you, this time when I'm sober enough to know exactly what I'm doing and why. Just say the word."

A small moan escaped her.

She couldn't help it. And he was right.

The urge to see him naked again was ridiculously strong. So maybe she was wrong about avoiding doing it again. Maybe if they banged it out of their systems, they could go back to being the platonic friends they had been before they succumbed to their desires. Neither of them were the type to get attached or addicted to their lovers, so it was only a matter of time until they both got this overwhelming desire out of their systems.

Maybe this was the only way to get back to square one.

Even as she talked herself into ignoring the warning signs yet again, a small voice in the back of her head wouldn't shut up. It kept asking…

But what if it made it *worse*?

"You're thinking too much," he whispered. "I wanna fuck you again. Do you want to fuck me?"

"Yes." She licked her lips. "And that's what scares me the most."

He backed her against the counter, his focus locked on her mouth. "Why does that scare you?"

"It just does."

He cupped her butt and lifted her up onto the counter next to her office, which had pens and paper scattered across it. Since she didn't use this surface for baking, she didn't stop him. "Because…?"

"When you're done with a woman, you walk away. You leave, and you don't come back. I don't want to lose you. I *can't* lose you," she said, opting for complete honesty. She'd stretched the truth once. She wouldn't do it again. "You mean too much to me. I wouldn't survive the loss. There would be a big, gaping hole in my world that would never be filled."

He buried his face in her neck, stepping between her legs. His hard erection brushed up against her, making it a lot harder to listen to those screaming warning thoughts. "What about if I promise—fucking *promise*—you won't lose me? I can. I do. I will never, *ever*, leave you, Lauren. I swear it."

She sucked in a deep breath. He didn't make promises. Didn't like the pressure, or the implied trap such a thing meant. So the fact that he did so, now, was not lost on her. And all the fight left her. He promised she wouldn't lose him.

And if she trusted him, which she did, and she still desired him, which she also did, what was holding her back? If she had nothing to lose…

What was stopping her?

Chapter Twelve

The internal battle she fought fleeted across her beautiful face. He'd struggled with it all night long, too, after she fell asleep. Even though he was being an even bigger asshole by giving in to his desire, nothing could stop him from doing it anyway. There was a hell of a lot at stake here, and he stood to lose everything…

But he could maybe gain a hell of a lot, too.

When he came here, he'd sworn he would keep his hands to himself. He had a plan. A course of action in place. Clean up his act. Keep his dick in his pants. Get the girl.

But then he got here, and she was beautiful, and all plans fled.

He *had* to have her.

"Lauren," he breathed, gripping her thighs. He stood between them, seconds from heaven, but she hadn't invited him in yet. "I'm gonna make you come, again and again. It's all I can think about ever since you kissed me. You. Me. Naked. Together. *Now*."

After what seemed like a million years, she nodded her

head. "Yes."

"Yes, what?" he said. He pressed against her again, his fingers digging into her thighs. "You have to say it."

She slid her hands down his chest and latched onto his sides right above his hips, in that same spot that he'd obsessed over on *her* all night long. "I want you. I'm all yours."

Growling, he captured her mouth, seizing the moment and refusing to let it go. She strained to get closer to him, but he held her firmly in place. His tongue entwined with hers, and he thrust against her. She moaned, and it drove him insane. It was just so damn sexy. After he left this morning, she put on a skirt, thank God, so he slid his hands up and inward, tracing her slit with his thumb.

She was wet and warm and ready—but she wouldn't get him.

Not yet.

First, he had to make her want it more than she ever wanted anything before. He drew a soft circle around her clit, soft enough to not send her over the edge, but hard enough to take her close enough to scream. She moaned and kissed him harder, her teeth digging into his bottom lip hard enough to draw blood, but he didn't give a damn.

All that mattered was getting her to scream his name again.

Shoving her panties aside, he thrust a finger inside her, crooking it just right. She dug her nails into his sides, groaning and arching her back. He ended the kiss, pressing his thumb against her clit, and pulled back. "So damn hot."

"*Steven.*" She slid her hands under his shirt, over his pecs, and scratched them down his abs. "I…I…nee—*ahhh.*"

"Shhh." He nipped her shoulder, taking his finger out of her heat before thrusting two inside her, hitting the spot guaranteed to make her let out that choked scream again. "You'll get it. All of it. I swear."

She gripped his pants, undoing the button with a flick of her wrist. "So will you. Let me—"

"Not yet. Not until I say so." He stilled her hand, like he always did when a woman tried to take control from him. "I'm—"

"Listen and listen now." Unzipping his jeans, she yanked him closer by them. "I'm okay with you being domineering in bed. It's sexy. And I'm okay with you holding me down sometimes, too, and telling me when I'm allowed to come. It turns me on. But, if I want to touch you? I'll do it." She tugged his pants down and closed her hand over his dick, squeezing with the perfect amount of pressure. "And you'll like it."

His gut twisted and all the blood in his body rushed south. Damn it, she was right. He *did* like it. He liked everything about her so much that he didn't even mind that she made him break all his rules—repeatedly. "Fuck, yeah."

She cocked a brow and closed her fingers over him, jerking him off with a light, feminine touch. His eyes rolled back in his head. "See? Told you."

Growling in reply, he kissed her again, harder this time.

She hesitated for a second, but kissed him back, her soft lips yielding to his with a sigh. He still had his fingers buried inside of her, so he pulled them out, thrusting them back inside. Touching her the same way she touched him.

She ran her fingers up his hard length and pumped her hips against his palm, letting out those sexy noises he loved so damn much. It made the desire to flip her over and fuck her from behind even stronger. But he continued teasing her, bringing her closer to the edge, but pulling back each time she got there.

And, damn it, she did the same thing to him.

By the time he nipped at her lip and ended the kiss, his breathing somehow matched her erratic breaths. "Enough," he growled, trapping her hand on his dick with his own. If she kept pulling and tugging and teasing, he'd be finished before they even started. "No more. It's my turn now."

She rested her weight on her palms and parted her legs wider for him. "Steven. *Yes*."

He knelt between her knees and nipped her thigh, his fingers still buried inside of her. He watched her as he fucked her with his hand. Her soft pink lips were wet and ready, and he ached to bury himself inside her. The strength of his desire for her would be enough to scare a lesser man. Maybe even him, if he let it. "It's only been a few hours, but shit, Lauren, I swear it's been too long since I was between your legs. I need another taste."

She spread her thighs wider, burying her hands in his hair, and let out a throaty chuckle. "Permission granted."

Heart pounding in his head, he tore her panties off, tossed them over his shoulder, and flicked his tongue over her swollen clit. She moaned and closed her legs on his head, holding him in place. He did it again, grinning when she squirmed, clearly trying to get closer, but he didn't let her. "You taste better than anything you've ever baked."

"Oh my God," she moaned. He froze. So did she. She shook her head. "Steven. I mean *Stev* — "

"Uh-uh," he said, pulling back. "Too late."

"Please don't stop," she begged, tightening her legs on his head and tugging on his hair roughly. "*Please*."

He didn't answer. Mostly because he didn't think he could. He was too busy trying to retain control over himself, and failing. No matter what she thought, the way she made him feel, and the things she did to him inside the bedroom and out of it, was unlike anything he'd ever felt or done before. She made him want to let go.

Forget himself, and all he'd done on the battlefield and off of it.

And that was a scary thought.

He closed his lips around her clit, sucking and licking until she screamed and rocked her hips against his mouth wildly, her breaths coming fast and hard. He couldn't get enough of her wild movements and breathy cries. They were simply too addicting.

She dug her heel into his upper back, arched her back, pressed closer to his mouth, and came. She screamed his name when she did, yanking on his hair as she soared, and ended on a sexy little moan that he loved. He didn't stop his torment, even though she bucked her hips and her cries of ecstasy turned into whimpers. He kept the strokes of his tongue light and teasing, and within moments, she was riding that train again, coming hard and sagging against the wall behind her.

That was his cue to move on to the next stop. By the time he was finished with her, she would never want to let him go. Standing, he grabbed her by the hips and flipped her over, so she stood in front of the counter with her ass in the air. Reaching into his pocket, he ripped open the foil packet he pulled out and rolled the condom on.

She was too spent to do much more than sigh and moan, so he slid her skirt up, baring her ass to his sight. "I'm not finished with you yet," he growled, palming her roughly.

She whimpered and pressed into his hand, despite her clear satisfaction with what he'd done to her so far. That was hotter than anything else she could have said or done. "*Steven.*"

"I'm here." He positioned the tip of his dick between her thighs, pressing inside of her just the slightest bit. "I'm not going anywhere. Not until I'm good and finished."

Whenever the hell *that* would be.

She scratched her nails across the stainless steel counter. "*Do it.*"

He cupped her from behind, resting his palm directly over her core. His fingers brushed her clit, and she sucked a deep breath in. "I will. When I'm fucking ready."

Slowly, lazily, he traced circles around her clit. She cried out, dropping her head on the counter, and fisted her hands. "You're *killing* me."

He chuckled throatily and pressed inside her a little more. "I'd never do that."

"Steven, I — " She let out a strangled groan, cutting herself off.

He thrust into her even more, his fingers still working over her sensitive clit. She screamed and reached behind her to grip his hips. "You were saying?"

She let out an unintelligible groan.

Then she slapped his ass. *Hard.*

And that made the last string that held his control break free. He thrust all the way inside her with one hard stroke. She screamed, and her tight pussy clamped down on him as she came immediately. He moved inside of her blindly, forgetting all about the world around them, or why it was so important he retain control.

All that mattered was this. Them. *Together.*

"*Lauren.*" He pumped his hips faster and harder, his fingers still working over her. She climbed higher with him, her hips moving frantically beneath him. When he gripped her ass, digging his fingers into the soft flesh, she came again.

And he was right there with her this time.

In fucking heaven.

He collapsed on top of her, his breathing harsh and fast, and tried to grasp his thoughts. They were all over the damn place. He'd let himself forget why it was so important he wait to make his move. He needed to make sure he could get his shit together before he took another step toward her.

Before he broke her heart.

Pushing off of her, he stepped back, swiped his forearm across his sweaty forehead, and swallowed hard. "Shit."

She glanced over her shoulder. "What's wrong?"

"Nothing," he said, not meeting her eyes.

What the *hell* was she doing to him? Just the sight of her draped across the counter, ass up, made him want another round. But he couldn't—shouldn't—take her until he knew he could clean up his act. Until he was certain he could be her man, in every way, without ruining everything.

So instead of touching her, he walked over to the trash, removed the condom, and ignored every instinct that told him to take more. As he pulled his pants up, the timer on the oven dinged. "Cake's done," he said drily.

"Steven…" She stood, pressing a hand to her chest as the other smoothed her skirt back into place. She was deliciously disheveled, with swollen lips and a loose ponytail. "What are we doing?"

He cocked a brow and tucked his semi-hard dick away. "Baking."

"That's not what I mean."

Instead of answering her, he remained silent. To be honest, he didn't have a damn clue. He'd had to have her. So he'd taken her. And he would do it all over again.

When it came to her, he had no self-control.

Once it became clear he wasn't going to answer, she gave him her back and strode over to the sink to wash her hands. He tried to get a read on her emotions and failed. When she shut the water off, she grabbed a towel and dried her hands, still not turning his way. She opened the oven door and bent down to check the cake, and it reminded him of earlier, which made his pulse race even more.

His thirst for her was ridiculous. They'd been friends for years without so much as a lingering touch, and now he simply couldn't get enough of her?

It made no sense…and yet it did.

He washed his hands. Even though he made sure not to

use a surface they needed for baking, he disinfected it after he was finished washing anyway. Anything to keep his hands busy, and his mind off of Lauren.

Something caught his eye, so he bent and picked it up. It was her tiny red lace panties. She was wrist deep in icing, so he shoved them in his pocket in case the customer decided to show up early. Then he walked up behind her, stopping just short of gluing his body to hers. Hesitantly, he reached out and rested his hands on her shoulders.

He still hadn't answered her, and she hadn't pressed him. She never did. But she deserved the whole truth, or he'd be no better than every other liar out there. He'd be a hypocrite. "The truth is, I don't have a clue what the hell we're doing."

She stilled beneath his palms. "Me either."

"I don't want to lie to you." He skimmed his thumbs over her soft skin. She felt so smooth under his calloused hands. All the shit he'd done and seen, and all the people he'd lost and saved, and this was the one thing that haunted him so deeply. This woman. "You never lie to me, so it only seems right to treat you with the same honesty you treat me."

She stiffened. "So don't. I don't need you to baby me, or worry about my feelings. I'm a big girl, and I know who you are. Even more importantly, who *I* am. And I don't need you, or any man, to be happy with myself. I don't—"

"I'm not babying you." He took a deep breath. "I'm lost."

"Aren't we all?" She continued stirring. Her long brown hair tickled his chin, and she still smelled like heaven, salvation, and temptation, all wrapped up into one irresistible package that was Lauren Brixton. "I can't remember the last time I thought I actually knew what I was doing with my life."

"But I can." He spun her around gently, and she fought him at first. But she gave in and faced him. The feelings in her eyes—the uncertainty, the fear, the *pain*—sent a shaft of those very same emotions piercing through him. "I'm fucked up right now. Have been since I came home. I've been happy, I've been sad, I've been hopeful, and hell, I'll admit it, I've been scared—but I've never been all of those things at once. Not until you kissed me."

She bit her lower lip. "Why?"

"When you're touching me, and I'm touching you, it just all…feels right." He ran his thumbs over the soft skin of her shoulders again, unable to resist. "But I don't want to break your heart, cupcake."

She rested her palms on his chest, one right over *his* heart. It sped up traitorously, showing her exactly how much she affected him. "Who said I was offering it to you in the first place? And if I was, then, whatever. It's my heart to guard, or not. That's my decision to make. Not yours."

"Shit." He dropped a kiss on her forehead. "I wasn't implying you were going to fall in love with me. I—"

"And yet, you kind of are." She frowned. "I don't see you worrying about your heart, or your feelings."

"I don't have one. It's why I can't stop myself from taking you, even though you deserve better, and it's why in the end, I might ruin what we have." He gritted his teeth. "And that's what pisses me off the most—my willingness to risk everything for another chance to be in your arms. But it won't stop me. I'm a selfish prick like that."

"Then I'll make it easy on you." She rested a hand on his palm, squeezing. "It's done. From now on…we go back to being friends. And only friends."

For a second, he felt relief. She'd given him an out, and he could—*should*—take it. Keep their friendship intact, and safe, and regain control. Be smart for once.

"No," he said slowly. Clearly.

She blinked at him. "No?"

"You heard me, cupcake."

"But you just said—"

"I know what I said, and it was the truth. It was. I wouldn't lie to you, just like you wouldn't lie to me." He tipped her chin up, and she blinked up at him, her cheeks going rosy. "I might not have a clue what the hell I'm doing, or how this ends, but I'm gonna fight for this—whatever the hell it is, or whatever it could be—because with you, I'm me. The real me. But first, I'm going to become a man who is worthy of you, and then I'm never gonna let you go."

And with that, he walked out into the sunlight. Right now…

He needed to fucking breathe.

Chapter Thirteen

After Steven's surprising admission earlier that day, followed by his hurried exit from her bakery, Lauren didn't know what to think anymore. He generally shied away from all intimacy and emotions of any sort—but he literally told her he was going to fight to keep her in his arms, no matter the ending to their story.

And that was *terrifying*.

There were a lot of other descriptions that suited the situation as well. Excitement, happiness, disbelief, uncertainty, and hope. But, yeah. Terrifying was the one emotion that stood out to her the most.

All these years, she kind of explained her inability to hold down a real relationship as Steven's fault. She'd refused to even entertain the idea of being with a guy long-term. No other man lived up to him, and he didn't want her, so it was okay that she didn't fall in love, or even want to.

The one man she could *maybe* love didn't love her back.

But if he was ready and willing to give them a try...and it failed? There was something wrong with her. If she couldn't love Steven, then she couldn't love *anyone.*

Lydia poked her in the ribs. "Hellllllo. Where are you right now?"

"Uh…" Lauren sat up straight and picked up her beer. "I'm here. I swear."

Lydia fluffed her hair and pressed the tips of her fingers to her mouth, looking a little thinner and a little bit green. She'd been sipping ginger ale while waiting for the men to arrive for dinner, instead of wine or her usual appletini, and Lauren was pretty sure why. The other woman looked way too happy to have contracted a stomach bug. "The other problem is, and I'm going to take a wild guess here…Steven."

Lauren laughed uneasily. "Why would you think that?"

"He's living with you, right?" At her nod, Lydia sighed. "What did the numbskull do now? Is he bringing too many girls back to your place already?"

Lauren's cheeks flushed. "I don't think you really want to go there with me. You're his sister."

"No, really?" Lydia smirked. "Is that why he was always hanging around my house without a shirt on all those years?"

"*Lydia.*"

The strawberry blonde shrugged. The fact that her hair was the same exact shade as Steven's never failed to escape Lauren's notice. "Spill it. What did my idiot brother do now?"

"Nothing. He did nothing at all." Lauren shredded the napkin in front of her on the wood table. "I'm not mad at him."

"I never said you were," Lydia corrected. "But he's staying with you, and you're being all quiet and pensive, so obviously something's going on. It's only safe to assume he's involved somehow."

Lauren remained silent.

After a while, Lydia sighed. "How'd you do it, by the way?"

"How'd I do what?"

"Get him to stay with you?" Lydia asked, pressing a finger against her red lips. "Did you make something up?"

Lauren shifted uncomfortably. "I had an ex come into my house and grab some stuff when I got out of the shower last night, and it freaked me out…so I asked him to stay. I exaggerated my level of fear a bit, so he agreed."

"Good thinking on your feet. And I really appreciate you doing this for us." Lydia twirled a piece of her hair on her finger. "And he won't find out about your…exaggeration. You're probably worried about that. I mean, with how much he values honesty, if he found out you lied—"

"He'd hate me." Lauren dropped the rest of her napkin. "Yeah, I know."

"I don't think he could ever *hate* you," Lydia said slowly. "He loves you too much for that."

"He doesn't love me," Lauren said quickly.

"Not like that. I didn't mean that," Lydia assured her. "You two are like bros, and that's how he loves you. He's told me that, like, a million times. I used to tease him about when the wedding would be, and he would get so mad."

Lauren forced a laugh. "Yeah. I get the same way."

"It's so cool that you two have managed to keep it platonic after all these years. Most people can't do that, and when they don't, it doesn't end well." Lydia scrunched her nose up. "I've seen it way too many times."

Lauren averted her eyes. "Yeah. Me too."

"But—" Lydia frowned and cut herself off. "Wait a second. Did something happen between you two? If so, I take it back. Forget I said any—"

"N-No. Of course not."

Lydia relaxed. "Good. That would make what's about to happen really awkward."

"Why?" Lauren blinked. "What's about to happen?"

"You know how last time you broke up with one of those jerks you date, and you were drinking, and you begged me not to let you pick another jerk?" Lydia swirled her straw in her soda. "And then you went and found another loser the next day?"

AKA Brian. Lauren stiffened. "Yeah…"

"Well, surprise." Lydia grinned. "You're single again, so I set you up on a blind date with a non-jerk before you could manage to find another one. And he's here. Now."

"Wait. What?" Lauren shook her head so fast the world blurred. "*No.*"

"Don't worry. He's great. Wait till you meet him." Lydia grinned mischievously. "Mark! Over here!"

"Don't do that," Lauren hissed, her cheeks going red-hot and her heart beating at a panicked pace. "Don't call him over here. I didn't agree to a freaking blind—"

"Glad you made it," Lydia said, her voice way too cheerful.

A man's shadow fell over them, and Lauren squeezed her eyes shut, unable to believe her luck. Why, of all nights, did Lydia have to pick tonight to follow through on that promise made over two months ago? It's not like she could announce she was currently sleeping with Steven, and therefore kind of, sort of, out of the dating pool. *Ugh.*

"Thanks for the invitation, Lydia." He paused. "And you must be Lauren?"

Forcing a smile, she turned to the man. "Nice to meet you, M—"

Lauren cut off. Mark was the hottest man she'd ever seen—besides Steven, anyway. He had light blond hair, dark brown eyes, and a body that had to have been sculpted from the gods. He wore a loose gray shirt, but nothing hid the muscles that screamed out to be noticed.

Steven was going to *flip.*

He grinned. Good God, he was even hotter when he did

that. "Mark."

"Right," Lauren said quickly. "Uh, Mark."

"It's nice to meet you. I work at the Shillings Agency, and just moved here from California."

So he worked with Steven. Even *better*.

"Crap," she blurted out, still distracted by his dazzling smile. When he looked confused, she forced a smile. She needed to lose this guy before Steven showed up. She had no idea where they stood, or what they were doing, but if he caught her talking to this guy—on a freaking *date*—he would understandably be upset. "Uh, I mean, cool. I bake things. In my bakery. That I own."

He laughed. "I like baked things. Where is this—?"

"It's on Chestnut, next to the bank," Steven said from somewhere behind her.

Of course he did. *Of freaking course.*

"Steven." She forced a smile, her heart racing. "Hi."

"What's up, cupcake?"

"Nothing," she squeaked.

He came up beside her, his gaze running down her body with a primitive possession burning in its depths before turning to Mark. "Lauren makes the best treats you'll ever taste. You should check it out sometime. I could take you after work, if you'd like."

"That would be great," Mark said, nodding.

Lauren blinked at Steven. He didn't *seem* jealous. Maybe she'd been putting way too much thought behind what he may or may not feel for her. And that bothered her more than it should have. "Thanks."

"She hand mixes everything to give it that homemade taste," Steven said, clapping Mark on the back. "Gives everything she touches one hundred percent of her attention. Isn't that right, Lauren?"

Lauren swallowed. "Uh…"

"How do you two know each other?" Mark asked, clearly confused.

"From school as kids," Steven said, his tone light. But then—oh God, then he frowned. And he gave her a long, searching look. "How did you two meet?"

She licked her lips. "I...uh, Lydia..." Crap. Her voice squeaked again. "Uh..."

"Your sister set us up on a blind date," Mark said slowly, staring at her strangely. She didn't blame him. "Lydia's your sister, right?"

All three of them slowly turned toward Lydia...who smiled and waved, clearly unaware of the tension among them. Holt grabbed Lydia and whispered something in her ear, gesturing wildly. Her mouth dropped open, and she shook her head.

"Yeah." Steven's jaw ticked. Twice. That was *not* a good sign. "She's my sister, all right." Then he stared at Lauren, fists tight at his sides. "And Lauren is my best friend."

He didn't lay claim to her. Didn't do some juvenile thing where he kissed her to show she was his, or throw his arm around her and pull her close. And yet, somehow...

He managed to do exactly that with a few words.

Lauren's heart palpitated. She couldn't look away from Steven, who held himself so tautly that it was a miracle he didn't break. "I just found out about this, Steven."

Mark, for his part, caught on to the tension quickly enough. He cleared his throat and shifted his weight to the balls of his feet. "You know what? I think I misunderstood her. There's clearly something going on between the two of you, and anyone with eyes can see that. Can I buy you both a drink to make up for all this confusion?"

Lauren blinked. "We're not...I'm not..."

"We're not together," Steven interjected, his jaw harder than ever before. "That's what you're trying to say, right,

Lauren?"

Lauren stared at him, not sure what she was *supposed* to say. It wasn't like they were going to announce to the world that they'd had sex a few times. It was no one else's business, and Lauren only assumed he wouldn't want to go around telling everyone.

Had she assumed *wrong*?

"I don't know what to say at all," she finally admitted.

The men stared at each other.

Stared each other *down*, was more accurate.

Mark smiled, even though it was clear he wished he'd never come up to Lauren in the first place. She didn't blame him. "So, about that drink?"

The silence stretched on for way too long *not* to be awkward, so Lauren cleared her throat. "I'd love a diet coke, Mark."

Mark shifted away from her immediately, the relief clear in his expression. "Great, I'll—"

"No. You stay," Steven said, his voice hard. "I'll get her a drink. I wouldn't want to interrupt your date." Steven turned on his heel and stalked off toward the bar without another word.

Well, *crap*.

Swallowing and forcing a smile, she turned back to Mark, who watched her closely. "So...misunderstanding, huh?"

"Yeah." He winced. "It seemed like the best excuse at the time. I had no idea you and Steven were a thing. I'm assuming Lydia doesn't, either."

"We're not. I mean, we are. But we're not." Lauren laughed and tucked her hair behind her ear. "It's, yeah. It's complicated."

Mark raised an impeccably shaped brow. "I got that."

"Yeah." Lauren laughed again. "I guess you did."

"Does *he* think it's complicated?" he asked, waving at

someone over her shoulder and smiling. Lauren glanced behind her, but there were only a few possibilities—all women. The only other person behind them was an old lady and a child. "Or does he think it's simple?"

"Yeah, I think so. But it just recently became... complicated."

Mark crossed his arms. "Ah. I see."

"Yeah..."

He laughed. "Well, if he's smart, he'll figure it out sooner rather than later." He grasped her shoulder and squeezed it. "You're gorgeous, and any man would be lucky to call you his."

Her cheeks heated. "Oh, stop it. You're too much."

"Stop what?" he asked, cocking that brow again.

"Being all cute and flirtatious and stuff." She patted his hand on her shoulder. "It won't work on me. Steven's got... well, me. I think."

"That's why I'm doing it. A little healthy competition never hurt anyone." He focused on something over her shoulder again, and his expression closed off. "But I don't think he agrees. He's coming over, and he looks pissed, so that's my cue to leave you two lovebirds alone. It was nice meeting you, Lauren."

She peeked over Mark's shoulder. Sure enough, Steven stalked over with her soda, and he looked ready to kill someone. "Oh God."

Mark laughed and walked away.

Way to abandon a girl, Mark.

When Steven reached her side, she held her hands up. "I didn't know anything about that, I swear—"

"Just drink your damn soda," Steven snapped, sliding it across the table to her. "I don't want to talk about it here, in front of everyone."

"I—" She barely managed to catch it before it hit the

floor. She'd been too busy watching him. The second she opened her mouth, he gave her a warning glare. "*Okay.*"

He turned away, his mouth tightening when Mark laughed at something Holt said. "Who the hell does that guy think he is, coming over here and flirting with you?"

So much for not talking about it.

"It wasn't his fault," she said.

"Wow, defending him already." Steven rolled his eyes, but his grip on the table was so tight it was a miracle it didn't break. "You liked him that much?"

"I barely know the guy. I'm just saying—"

"You knew him well enough to flirt with him," he snapped.

"I never—!" She blinked. "Wait a second. Are you... *jealous?*"

He snorted. Actually snorted. "I don't fucking get jealous. If he wants to come over here and flirt with you, then he can. I'm not going to stop him, or you. It's a free country. I did my share of fighting to keep it that way—and so did he."

She bit down on her tongue so hard it brought tears to her eyes. He was being ridiculous in his denial, but if she laughed like she was about to, he'd get angry. And if he got angry, they would fight. And if they fought, everyone would figure out why.

But if he wasn't jealous, then she would run down the street naked.

In daylight.

After she pulled herself together, she said, "Be angry all you want, but it's not my fault that your sister decided to throw a handsome, single stranger my way—"

"*Handsome?*" He growled and grabbed her hand, hauling her after him and toward the door. As they passed Holt and Lydia—who both watched them with wide eyes and open mouths—he said, "We forgot something out in the car. We'll be right back."

Lauren tugged on her hand. "*Steven.*"

"No." The second they went outside, away from prying eyes, he pressed her against a wall, melding his hard body against hers. "You think he's fucking *handsome*?"

"I…" She gasped and placed her hands on his chest. He slid his leg in between hers and pressed a knee against her core. "What are you doing?"

"Touching you. Claiming you." He lowered his face to hers, stopping just shy of kissing her. "Making you forget all about him, and reminding you why you shouldn't have given him a second glance in the first place."

Her stomach hollowed out, and she swallowed hard. He was being all possessive and domineering and…yes, *jealous.* She didn't normally like jealousy on a man, but on Steven, it looked good. "I wasn't even looking at him. I was looking at you."

"Good." He rolled his knee against her clitoris, slowly and tortuously. "I don't like the idea of you wanting some other guy. I've never been so angry before. I've never been so—so—"

Her mouth quirked up. She couldn't help it. "Jealous?"

His brows slammed down. "Hell no. I'm not—" Comprehension lit his expression, and he tightened his grip on her waist. "*Shit.* Yes, damn it. I'm fucking jealous. I've never wanted to claim a woman as mine, and all mine, as much as I did tonight."

His "claim" on her was primitive and outdated, but even so, she liked it. The possession in his hold and voice made her nipples tighten, and she pressed against his knee. A gasp escaped her at the friction. "*Steven.*"

"I'm here, cupcake. And I'm not going *anywhere.*" He buried his hands in her hair and tugged until her face pointed up toward his. "Got it?"

The meaning behind those words was not lost on her. He

echoed his promise from earlier, and she believed him. "Got it," she breathed.

He let out a sexy growl and kissed her. The second their lips touched, it was like fireworks went off in the street, bursting all around them. His hands ran over her curves, touching everywhere...but not enough. She clung to his shoulders, tongue entwining with his, and moved against his knee, each stroke taking her higher and higher.

Everything else—the worries, the doubts, the confusion, and the fear—faded away in his arms. Her entire body tightened. God, she was close. So close that her fingers tingled and her stomach tightened. One more thrust and—

Without warning, he broke the kiss off and took his knee back. "That's all you get, after what happened inside," he said, his voice strained. "We'll finish this when we get home—after we talk."

"*Steven*," she managed to get out. She drew in a ragged breath. "Please."

She'd pulled that out into play out of desperation. It worked every other time. But apparently...not this one. He didn't kiss her again. Just stared.

"No." He rested his forehead on hers, gripping her hips and fisting her shirt there. "Not until we figure out what the hell we're doing, but it's not going to happen here, when my sister and Holt are waiting for us to come back inside."

He hauled her close again, slamming his mouth down on hers.

When he pulled back, they both gasped for air, clinging to one another.

It was a lot harder to let go of him than it should have been. She took a shaky breath. "This is crazy. For years, you didn't even look at me like that. But now I can't stop kissing you, and—"

"That's not true," he argued. "I *looked*. The difference

between then and now is that I see exactly who and what we are—and what we could be."

She fisted his shirt. "Steven, I'm not—"

"Don't. Don't say anything yet." He pressed a finger to her mouth, his hazel eyes warm and pulling her under his spell. "Just think about it. About us. Okay?"

Oh, she'd think about it, all right.

In fact, she wouldn't be able to think about anything *else*.

Chapter Fourteen

Steven glanced at Lauren with his peripheral vision. The moonlight played with the highlights in her hair, and softened her beautiful features. She'd been quiet all night, and he had no clue if that was a good thing. He'd been honest, and open, and if he fucked himself over by doing so?

It was too late to take it all back now.

The truth about his feelings was out.

He had to wait to see if she felt the same way about him. And if, by some miracle, she did, then he had to try like hell not to screw it up, like he had with Rachel. But with Lauren, he had to have faith he would keep his shit together.

That this time would be different.

Or he was even more of a screwup than he originally thought.

They walked up to her house, hand in hand, neither one of them speaking as they climbed up her stairs and into her townhome. She closed and locked the door behind them, flicked the switch on, and those bright blue eyes locked on him. "You didn't drink tonight."

"I know." He smiled. She seemed genuinely happy. And that's all he could ask for right now. Her smiling. "You lectured me. I listened. Are you really that surprised?"

"Kind of." She brushed her hair out of her face, tucking it behind her ear. "You never really listened to me before. Why now?"

He was trying to "show" her he cared about her, that he could be the right kind of man for her, and doing his damnedest not to mess it up. "You deserve better than a drunken guy in your bed. You deserve a prince." He frowned and rubbed his jaw. "No. Fuck that. That's not good enough. You deserve a king."

She swallowed so hard it filled the silence of the room. "So do you."

"I don't like kings," he teased, running his finger down her arm. Goose bumps rose, and she shivered. "I like brunettes who tell me to get my shit together, and stop being an asshole. So I'm trying."

She smiled, her whole face lighting up. Hell, it even made him feel like he was brighter. Happier. And that was something a guy couldn't take for granted. "And apparently I like men who get me close to an orgasm…and then stop."

"Touché." He laughed. "I promised to finish later, though."

"After we talk," she said cautiously, kicking off her heels. "So. Talk."

Sighing, he sat on the couch and kicked his boots off. Shit. It was D-Day, and he still didn't have a speech prepared. He'd been agonizing over it all night, but the words wouldn't come. He wasn't kidding earlier. She deserved a king, and if he had any chance of winning her over, he had to find a way to become one. For her.

So he settled for: "How did the cake pick-up go?"

"Uh, good." She blinked, clearly at a loss by his evasion. But he needed time to make it right in his mind. This was too important to wing it. "They loved it."

"Of course." He clasped his fingers behind his neck. "You made it. What's not to love?"

She didn't say anything to that.

In fact, she remained completely silent.

After a while, he cracked an eye open. She watched him, still holding her purse, one shoe off and one shoe on, still standing right by the door as if scared to move. "What's up?"

"You're acting...weird." She hesitated. "You seem different. Kind of like...the old you. Not that the current you is bad or anything. But you didn't drink. And you're relaxed, and teasing me, and it's *nice*."

"It's because of you." He sat forward and held a hand out for her. To his surprise, she didn't hesitate. She came over and placed hers inside his trustingly. "Like I said, around you, *with* you, I am different. I'm *me* again."

Her cheeks flushed with color. "Why? Is it because we... you know?"

"I already answered a question." He forced a smile. "Now it's your turn."

She smirked, amusement coming to life in those beautiful eyes of hers. They hadn't played Truth or Dare since college, but it seemed fitting tonight. "Oh, we're playing *that* game, huh?"

"Yep." He smoothed her hair out of her face and bopped her on the nose. It was so tiny and cute. "Truth or dare. You answer honestly, or you succumb to a dare."

A small laugh escaped her, and she sat down beside him, curling her foot under her ass as she turned to face him. "Why do I get the feeling this is going to get a heck of a lot dirtier than it was ever meant to be?"

Well, if that's the way she planned to play, he wouldn't complain. But he had a different game in mind. One that showed her just how serious he was about her. He might not be good enough for her, but he'd spend the rest of his life *trying* to be, and that had to count for something. Right?

But still, some small part inside of him felt guilty for how happy she made him. The men on his team wouldn't get the chance to be this happy. They'd never get to hold a woman in their arms, or fall asleep with a warm body pressed against them.

Why should *he*?

"Do you think I want it to be dirty?" he replied.

She rolled her eyes. "You're Steven. Of course you do."

For some reason, this made him laugh. He laughed so hard his sides hurt, and then he laughed some more. And Lauren? Yeah, after staring at him with wide eyes at first, she laughed just as hard, and just as loud, as he did. And it felt fucking *amazing*. He didn't remember the last time he'd been so amused, and truth be told? He wasn't sure he ever had been.

This, right here? *This* was all he needed to be happy. His Lauren. He'd been a fool not to see it all along.

"Shit," he said, swiping the tears of laughter off his cheeks. When he glanced at her, she was red and breathing heavily, her cheeks wet. Smiling, he smoothed his thumbs over her soft skin, drying hers, too. They locked eyes, and for the life of him...

He couldn't look away.

Slowly, her gaze dipped down to his mouth, and her lids drifted shut. It would be so easy to kiss her. To forget all about the future, and defining who they were, and figuring their shit out before they got naked again. So damn *easy*.

But for once in his life, he didn't want to do that.

He wasn't looking for a quick fix or an orgasm.

So he pulled back. "Your turn to ask a question."

"Oh. I guess that was a question, huh?" She licked her lips, her small pink tongue darting out to tease him, making his decision to be good even harder. "Okay, uh…did you like baking today?"

"Yeah." He chuckled at her question. "It was all right, but I liked what we did on the counter even more."

She bit down on her lower lip. "Me too."

His dick hardened even more in protest at all this *talking*. "My turn." He took a deep breath. "Are you too scared to take a chance on me?"

She fidgeted. "I…no." She paused. "I don't think I am."

Relief filled him, and he couldn't help it. He leaned in and pressed his mouth to hers, kissing her with all the excitement that filled him at her answer. When he pulled back, he trailed his knuckles down the side of her face and smiled. She smiled back.

"Ask me anything." He pulled her against his body. There was a moment where she stiffened, and he was sure she would push away from him. She didn't. Instead, she curled up against him like that was where she belonged all along. "I'll answer."

She rested a hand on his heart. It sped up. "You said that you finally felt like you, for the first time in forever, when I kissed you. I wasn't aware that had changed."

Silently, he thought about it. *Really* thought about it. "I wasn't, either, until last night, when you were sleeping. That's when it hit me. I haven't been myself since I came home. Since I left my team, and the SEALs."

"Oh." She tipped her face up to his, staring at him with so many unasked questions. And, oddly enough, he was ready to answer them all. To finally open himself up to someone, completely, and trust that it wouldn't come back to bite him in the ass. "Do you miss it?"

"Every damn day," he admitted. "Sometimes, I'm not sure how to be me without my team behind me, watching my back. And the reason I lost them haunts me every day and night. I dream about them. About what I could have done differently."

She shook her head sadly. "You can't do that to yourself."

"Yeah, I can. It was my fault." He pinched the bridge of his nose. He'd never admitted it out loud before, but it was true. "And that's all I'm gonna say on that matter."

She stiffened, going a little bit pale. "I don't believe you."

He closed his eyes, reliving that day in hell. Gunshots sounded in his head, and blood splattered on the dirt and sand in front of him, and the screams of his men filled his head. When his superior told him it was a raid to check for any ammunition in an abandoned warehouse, Steven sensed something was off with his story.

But he hadn't called him on it.

"Well you should. I killed them." He swallowed hard. "I killed them all. It was my fault."

He could still hear Morgan as he shouted it was a trap. He hadn't finished his sentence before a bullet hit him in the throat.

He choked on his own blood, and no one had been able to save him.

Not even Steven.

The rest had fallen, all around him, and the only one to walk away from that fucked up day had been him. To this day, he still couldn't figure out why.

He should have died, too.

If he had called his superior out on his lie, they would still be here today. And he would still be with them, keeping them safe.

"Steven…"

A tear escaped her eye, and she quickly wiped it away like she didn't want him to see. Too late. A part of him wished he could cry, too. Grieve. Move on.

But he never would.

"My turn," he said quickly, interrupting her. He'd talked

about that day long enough. He needed to clear his brain. Quiet the screams of his men. But still, even though it was hard to talk about, with her, it didn't feel so bad.

With her, it was *freeing*.

If anyone else had asked, he wouldn't have been so honest. He would have said it was time to leave his position in the SEALs, or that he'd been ready to move on, all the bullshit he usually spat out when people asked him questions like that. But the truth was, he'd been forced out by a well-placed shot that limited his ability to aim and shoot properly. So...it had been a desk job or retirement.

He hadn't been ready to leave.

Hadn't wanted to be *normal*.

But here he was, trying his best to do those things anyway.

And Lauren made that all a little easier. He massaged her back in slow, sweeping circles. "I've asked you this before, but we're older now, and I have a feeling your answer changed. What's your biggest fear?"

She shifted her weight uneasily. "Wow. That's a tough one. I guess...it would be dying alone. Dad left when I was a baby, and Mom died right after high school. Even before that, I barely even saw her. But if everyone else gets married and moves on with their lives, and I'm all alone...yeah. I would be the old lady that dies and no one finds out till after her cat eats half her rotting, smelly, exploding flesh away."

He laughed. He couldn't help it. "Wow. That's quite the image you paint."

"It's the truth." She placed a hand over his shoulder, where the scar from his injury was. The one that ended his career. "My turn again. If you hadn't been shot, would you still be there now?"

"It's the only place I've felt like I had a meaning to my life. The only place I've felt like I belong, and that I knew what my purpose was." He rested his hands on hers and held on to it. "So, yeah, I'd be over there, fighting and serving my country. It pisses me off that I can't anymore. I feel useless. Like my entire life has nothing left to it anymore."

She reared back. "That's insane. You're a valuable part of the Shillings Agency. And you have Lydia. Holt. Your parents." She hesitated. "Me."

"Do I?" he asked. "Sometimes, it doesn't feel like it."

"Steven…"

He took a deep breath. "My turn. Why do you think you'll be alone? Why are you so sure no one will fall in love with you, or ask you to marry them?"

"Quite frankly…" She bit down on her tongue. He could see it. "I'm not sure I'm capable of the kind of love that other people feel."

He stilled. "Why not?"

"It's my turn, not yours. Why do you want to be with me all of a sudden?"

"I can't think of anything else." He traced an invisible path on his knee, frowning down at it. "I didn't let myself think about it before, but you kissed me. And everything changed. Now I want to be with you so badly it hurts. Why did you kiss me last night?"

She swallowed hard. "I always wondered what it would be like. Why did you kiss me back?"

"I needed to kiss you, too," he shot back. "Was it what you imagined?"

"Even better." She licked her lips, and he couldn't look away from the wet sheen she left behind. "So much better. Why have you been drinking so much?"

Shit. She had to ask him that. Had to throw it out there. "It helps me forget I lost my way. And it makes me forget all the people I didn't save. And the ones I no longer can save. How many people do you think die, every day, over there, that I could have saved if only I was still there? I don't think I want to know. But it haunts me. If I'd—" He broke off, not wanting to tell her about the lie that ended his career, and his friend's lives. "It's just, if things had played out differently, everything could be different. And those men would still be with their families."

"When Lydia called me in the middle of the night, I was terrified she was calling to tell me you were dead." She fisted his shirt and took a deep breath. "It was, hands down, the most frightening moment of my life. When she told me you were alive, I sat down and I couldn't move. Not even after we hung up."

Swallowing hard, he hugged her, still rubbing her back. Funny, but he never really thought about that. What it would be like to be on the other end of the phone, getting that call. He tried to imagine how he would feel if the roles were reversed, and it didn't feel good at all. He kissed the top of her head, taking a second to breathe in her sweet scent. "I'm sorry."

She didn't say anything, but snuggled closer.

It was his turn, so he asked, "Why did you ask me to stay here?"

"I...uhh..." Lifting her head, she opened her mouth, going pale. Fear flashed across her eyes, and she shook her head once. "Dare. I'll take a dare."

Out of all the questions, that wasn't the one he expected her to avoid. What was so damn bad that she had to hide it from him? That she refused to answer? "Seriously? That's the one you don't want to answer?"

"Yep." She didn't so much as waver from her decision. "What's my dare?"

"Give me a chance to be more than a friend to you. Let me be your lover. Your friend. The person you come home to at night, the one who holds you when you're upset. The guy who needs you as much as you need him." He locked eyes with her. "Let me be yours, and say you're mine."

She didn't say anything. Just stared.

And stared some more.

She was silent for so long that he was tempted to snap a finger in her face to jerk her out of whatever world she currently resided in. But just as he was about to, she opened her mouth. "I want to. I do," she said, wringing her hands in front of her chest. "I just… It scares me. The idea of losing you."

"I told you." He cupped her face and offered her a small smile. "I'm not going anywhere, cupcake. Even if you break my heart, I'll be right here. At your side."

She shook her head slightly, pressing her face closer to his palm. Turning, she kissed it. Her touch lingered even when she faced him again. "I believe you. I do. But you're you, and I'm me…"

"And you don't think we could make it work," he said flatly.

She bit down on her lip hard. "Do you?"

"I do." He ran his hand down her neck and over her back till he rested right above her ass. "I really fucking do. I think we could be happy. If you let me, I think I could spend the rest of my life trying to make you smile and laugh." His mind wandered to what he'd seen earlier, on her nightstand. She had a glass jewelry box, so when he'd been pacing and thinking, he'd seen it. Sitting there. Plain as day. "Do you remember what we promised each other after I came home from my first tour?"

She gaped at him for so long he gave up on getting an answer from her. Maybe she didn't remember. Maybe he was the only one that clung to long ago spoken words that meant so much and yet—

"Yeah." She cleared her throat. "We said we would get married if we were both single when you were thirty." She scooted away from him, shrugging out of his hold, and hugged her knees, watching him warily. "You remember that?"

"Of course I remember it."

They locked gazes, neither one moving.

Finally, she gripped her calves tighter and spoke. "Why are you mentioning this now? That was a lifetime ago."

"I've been thinking about it. A lot."

She gave a nervous laugh. "But *why*?"

"I think I said those things for a reason. Something I wasn't sure of, or even wanting to consider, but I think when I asked you to marry me if we were both single, it was because I had a feeling this moment would come. That when we were both ready, you'd be mine, and I'd be yours, and it would just be right." He cleared his throat. "I saw it in your jewelry box this morning. I didn't open it or anything, but it was resting right on the top, inside the glass lid. You kept the ring. Why?"

She covered her face. "Oh God."

"*Lauren*."

"I couldn't get rid of it," she whispered. "It was a silly thing, and we were drunk, but to me...it was special. And I didn't want to forget that moment, so I kept it. It's not a big deal or anything. Just a keepsake."

He swallowed. It had been special to him, too. He just hadn't realized it till now, almost nine years later. "I'm single, and thirty."

"Don't." She hopped up, covering her mouth with a trembling hand. "You can't be serious right now. We had sex twice. Twice. That doesn't mean we should get married."

"Jesus." He stood, too, and held his arms out. "I'm not asking you to *marry* me, for fuck's sake. I'm not that much of an asshole. If I ever asked anyone to marry me, it would be a hell of a lot better than this moment."

She lowered her hand. "What *are* you asking me?"

"The same thing I already asked for. Be my girlfriend. For

the first time in forever, I found a new purpose. It's to make you happy. To make you laugh so hard you have to clutch your stomach. To brighten your life up, and to let you do the same to mine. To be your *person*."

"You're already my person," she said, smiling. Her eyes watered. "My best person."

"But I want to be more. To be everything." He grabbed her hands and squeezed. "You and I? We make sense. It's why I made that silly promise all those years ago. Tell me I'm wrong."

She sucked in a deep breath. "I want to be with you more than you'll ever know, which is what scares me so much, Steven. *So. Much.*"

"That's when it's right. When it scares the shit outta you."

She eyed him. "You don't get scared of anything."

"Correction. I didn't." He squared his jaw. "But then I woke up in your bed, and I realized that this thing between us could work out, and just how much I stood to lose if it didn't."

She swallowed. "So you're scared of me?"

"Hell yeah. You terrify me."

A strangled laugh escaped her. "I feel the same way about you."

"Is that a yes?"

She nibbled on her lip, watching him. This moment, no matter what her answer might be, was going to be engrained in his memory for the rest of his life. Her soft blue eyes shone brighter than a summer's day sky. Her plump, pink lips parted as she breathed, and a fetching pink flushed her cheeks.

And then she smiled, and his heart sped up

"Steven…" She licked her lips, and nodded. Fucking *nodded*. "Yes. I'll be your girlfriend." She launched herself into his arms and kissed him.

And for the first time in months…

He wasn't lost.

Chapter Fifteen

"This literally makes no sense." Lauren crossed her arms, staring at the TV with narrowed eyes. "He's in a box, and it just shows up in London—heck, all over the world, and no one finds it odd that at one moment, there's a random police box outside their homes, and the next day…it's gone? And no one reports it?"

Steven laughed. "Would you call the cops if there was a police box down the road from your place?"

"I—" A robotic human thing walked down the roads of London, and no one even screamed. "What even *is* this? I'd freak out if I saw that thing, that's for sure!"

Two nights ago, she had lost a bet with Holt, and her price had been agreeing to one full night of a *Doctor Who* marathon with Steven. They were on their second episode, and it still made absolutely no sense whatsoever. And the aliens were creepy.

Holt and Steven had set her up.

She never stood a chance of winning that bet.

"Can we just tell Holt we watched it?" She leaned in

and traced a path down his happy trail, dropping her voice seductively. "I can think of better things to do…"

Steven laughed even harder and caught her hand. "Not a chance."

"Ugh." She flopped back against the couch dramatically. "This suuuucks."

He shook his head. "You're thinking about it way too much. You're supposed to get lost in the characters, and sympathize with the sad plight of the Doctor."

"What's so wrong with his life?" she asked, gesturing to the screen. "He flies around in a box that's bigger on the inside, saving planets and lives, with a human companion that loves him. It sounds pretty great to me."

"He's the last of his kind. The last Time Lord to ever fly in a TARDIS." Steven paused, and his smile slipped away. "And even worse, it's all his fault that he's the last one. He killed them to save the universe."

Lauren swallowed hard, eyeing Steven.

His tone was casual, but the way he held his knees was anything but. He flexed his jaw and stared at the screen. Judging from the distant expression in his eyes, he wasn't even here with her. He was in another time, and another place, when he'd lost all his men, too. And from what little he'd told her, he blamed himself.

She wasn't sure what happened over there, but she knew one thing.

Those deaths weren't his fault.

"How did he kill them all?"

Steven shifted. "He blew up his planet to stop the time war. All Daleks and all the people of Gallifray died. And he did it. He pushed the button."

"Wow." She rested a hand on his shoulder. "Is that why you sympathize with the Doctor? You're the last ones left?"

His jaw flexed. "Yes, and we're both guilty as hell."

"Steven—"

"Don't." He pinched the bridge of his nose. "You have no idea what happened over there, and I'm not telling you, so drop it."

She bit her tongue. "Those men you lost. They were friends. Right?"

"Brothers." He rested his head against the couch, staring up at her. What lurked in those depths—anger, pain, confusion, *guilt*—twisted her stomach in knots, and made her heart ping in sympathy. "All of them."

She nodded, running her thumbs across the stubble on his cheeks. "And you loved them." It wasn't so much of a question as it was a statement. After all, she already had her answer. A man who grieved so thoroughly for someone else obviously cared.

He squared his jaw, not answering.

It was enough.

"So do you think they'd want you to continue punishing yourself, and blaming yourself? Would they expect you to live the rest of your life alone and shut off from any emotion, because you lived and they died?" she asked, keeping her voice soft.

His nostrils flared, and he took an uneven breath. "I don't know, but it's what I was determined to do." He slowly slid his hand up her side, leaving a trail of tingling skin in his wake. "What I *was* doing—right up until you kissed me."

"And now?" she asked, her breath hitching in her throat.

"Now I feel too much," he admitted, going over her shoulder, across her chest, and burying his fingers in her hair. "I'm alive again, and happy, and it's because of you. You showed me how to live again, and I don't want you to ever stop."

"I won't," she whispered. "I promise."

"Don't make promises. No one ever keeps them," he said,

his voice gruff.

"I do." She ran her thumb over his lower lip. "I will."

"Lauren. *My* Lauren."

With a grimace, he pulled her face down to his and kissed her. They'd kissed a lot of times, in lots of different ways, over the last few days. But this time felt...*new*.

Like maybe, just maybe, he was starting to believe in her. And himself.

Four days later, Lauren woke up slowly with a smile on her face. After their serious conversation about him forgiving himself, they'd opted for lighter conversation. And there had been laughing. *So much laughing.* He fulfilled one part of his promise to her—he made her belly hurt.

And it had been glorious.

Ever since she agreed to be his, he'd been the Steven he had been before he left for war. The one who joked around and spoke openly about everything. The man she fell for so long ago, when they'd been nothing more than children, and she was falling harder and faster now, as an adult.

Being with him was like a rush. Like riding a roller coaster when it's approaching the top of the first hill. Just as it was about to plummet down, and she was going to scream, and her stomach was about to fly up in her throat. And when it was over, she was ready to get right back on and do it again.

She rolled over and reached out for him, but the bed was empty. Her lids drifted open lazily, and she searched the room. His shoes were gone, and so were his clothes. There was a note on the pillow.

Had to go to work early this morning. I couldn't bear to wake you after keeping you up all night, so I didn't. I'll see you tonight. Save me some red velvet cupcakes.

Steven

She smiled down at the writing, which was messy and scribbled at best. Next to it, he'd placed the twist tie. Their promise ring. She snatched it up, rolled out of bed, and put it back in the jewelry box.

As she closed the lid, she glanced at herself in the mirror. Her hair was a mess, and she looked like she hadn't slept in a week, but she was...

Really, truly, *happy*.

As she showered, she whistled and washed, smiling at all the sore spots she discovered. And when she got to work at ten minutes before seven, she smiled at every customer who came in a little more widely than usual. Buying this bakery had been the biggest leap of faith she ever made—up until the other night when Steven asked her to be his.

That had been an even bigger one.

But the thing about leaps was, if you landed safely on the other side, you looked over your shoulder at what you left behind on the other side, and then looked forward at the beauty of the new, undiscovered side. And then you started your life all over again.

With the person or thing you took a leap with.

And doing it with Steven had been the best decision she ever made.

At six o'clock on the nose, her phone dinged. It was a text from Steven. Her heart accelerated. When she read it, she laughed out loud.

I need some sugar, baby.

Red velvet, right?

His reply was immediate.

I meant you, but sure. That works, too. I'll take both. I'm greedy like that.

She laughed.

Ha. You're funny.

The bubble with three dots popped up instantly.

Are you gonna leave me standing out here all night long, or are you gonna let me in?

She lifted her head. Sure enough, waiting on the opposite side of the locked glass door was Steven.

Oh. Hi.

He held up a bouquet of red roses.

Let me in?

Maybe…

He crossed his arms and smirked at her.

Grinning, she opened the door and he came inside. "Before you get any ideas, I already cleaned up for the night. So no hanky-panky on the counter."

"Hanky-panky?" he said, laughing. And that laugh? Yeah, it did things to her heart. Dangerous things. If only she could spend the rest of her life making him laugh like that. "Did you seriously just use that in a sentence?"

"I did." She tried not to smile…and failed. "And I rocked it."

"That's a subjective statement. You rock those shorts. You rock being naked." He gave her a once-over. "Hell, you rock pretty much anything you do—but that sentence? Yeah, I'm not so sure that applies."

"Hey." She smacked his arm. "You better watch yourself, or you'll be sleeping on the couch."

That smirk slid off his face real fast. "Shit. You can hold that over my head now. No one's ever been able to do that to me."

"Not even Rachel?"

"I didn't like sleeping in the same bed as her." He shot her a quick glance and lowered his head. "I had nightmares when I first came back, and she didn't…handle them well. Let's just put it that way."

Nightmares. Of course he did.

And of course little miss prissy Rachel couldn't handle them. She'd never been the right girl for Steven. She was too soft. Too sensitive. Too childlike in her selfishness.

Steven needed a real woman. One who could love him for his faults, not in spite of them. Who could love him equally in his good nights, and his bad. Who would never give up on him, or ever stop fighting for him. Someone who would love him unconditionally for the rest of his life, no matter what he said or did.

Someone like…*her*.

Lauren swallowed hard, but forced a smile. "If you ever need me to be there, anytime, anyplace, I'll chase the nightmares away."

He stared at her, as if he wasn't sure what to say or do.

Then, without warning, he pulled her into his arms and kissed her, keeping it soft and short. His hard lips on hers still made her knees weak, though.

"Thank you," he whispered, staring down at her.

He still held the flowers in his hand.

"For what?" she asked, her breath coming light and fast.

"For always being honest with me, and for being someone I can trust enough to let in." He skimmed his fingers over her jawline. "You have no idea what that means to a guy like me.

If I didn't trust you, there's no way I could let you...that I could open myself up like this. So, thank you."

She sucked in a breath and held it in. Those words were everything she'd wanted to hear, and more. And she needed a second to really, truly let that sink in.

"Are you okay?" he asked, his brow furrowed.

"Y-Yes, sorry." She smiled up at him, resting her hands on his chest. "I was...thinking how happy I am right now. With you."

"The feeling is mutual." He pulled back and handed her the flowers. She took them and lifted them to her nose, inhaling deeply. "Will you go out with me?"

"I thought we already were." She blinked at him over the bouquet. "If not, these past few days I've spent rolling around naked with you are really confusing."

A laugh burst out of him and punched her right in the chest. Looking at him, she realized he was more than her friend and lover. He was the love of her life.

She *loved* him.

"I mean, like *out*," he said, ripping her out of her frightening thoughts. But the thing was, they weren't all that scary. They should have been, but for some reason, it just felt...right. "Sitting at a table together. With each other."

"You mean, on a date?"

"Yeah." He tucked her hair behind her ear for her. "Our first real date."

Setting her flowers down, she walked around the counter and pulled out a cupcake. "I'd love to...but first...you need to eat a cupcake."

He smirked. "I love eating...*cupcakes*."

"Oh my God, you're incorrigible," she said with red cheeks. "Eat your dessert."

He cocked a haughty brow. "Before dinner?"

"You'd best get used to that," she teased, handing him a

cupcake. He took it, his fingers purposely catching hers as he tugged her back into his arms. It was as if he couldn't bear to have her out of them—and, again, the feeling was mutual. "I plan on giving my kids sweets whenever they want, too. Life's too short to wait for the good stuff."

He stilled. "…Kids?"

Well, crap. She was dating him—actually *dating* him—and she'd mentioned the "k" word on their first real date. But she already had deep feelings for this man. It wasn't a huge shock that she might go there. If she could get that happy ending with anyone, with the kids and the dog and the fenced-in yard, it would be him.

But that didn't mean he felt the same way.

She stuttered. "I-I-I mean, you know. If I have them someday. Which I might not. I'd probably be a horrible mom."

His gaze dipped down to her belly, and when he studied her face, there was something that looked like…longing. As if he, too, thought about it, and liked the idea. "I think you'd make an awesome mother someday."

Lauren forced a light laugh. "Yeah, we'll see. So…dinner?"

"Yeah. Right. Uh, I made reservations." He finished his treat, dusted off his hands, and held his arm out for her. He still wore a suit from his day at the office, while she had on shorts and a tank top. "Are you ready?"

"Depends. Do I need to change?"

"Why would you do that?" He frowned. "You look beautiful already. You always do."

Her heart skipped a beat at the compliment. "Well, if we're going somewhere fancy, I need to wear a dress."

"Nah, you're fine." He opened the door for her, and led her through it. "Lock up."

She did. The whole time, she felt his gaze on her.

There was something there, buried in those hazel depths that made her heart race and her thighs tremble. When she finished, she turned to him. He pressed her against the door, towering over her, his chest pressed to hers, and trapped both her hands on either side of her body. She almost dropped the flowers. "Steven?"

"You look so damn pretty in the moonlight. How did it take me so long to see what was right in front of me? How could I have been so damn blind?"

He lowered his mouth to hers, stopping just shy of kissing her. His warm, minty breath fanned across her cheek. Tears threatened to spill out. Not from fear—though she was scared, too—but he looked down at her as if she was the most important thing on this planet, and she had no idea what to *do* with that. She'd never been anyone's first choice. Never had someone who literally needed her in his life.

Her mother had been too busy mourning the loss of her father for her entire life while paying bills, so Lauren had always been on her own. No one needed her. But Steven…he *did*. And that meant a lot to her. So much.

She didn't want to lose it, or him.

A tear slipped out, and Steven's thumb caught it with lightning fast reflexes. "Why are you crying? I didn't want to make you cry. Shit, I'm sorry, cupcake."

He'd freed one of her hands, so she curled it behind his nape and shook her head again, gasping for a good breath. The emotion inside of her was…was…*overwhelming*. "I'm not crying."

"Uh…" He tried to pull back, but she didn't let him. "Then what the fuck is coming out of your eyes?"

"Tears. But they're good ones. *Very* good." She took a deep breath. "I—"

"In that case?" He brushed his lips across hers lightly. "I can make them happier."

She curled her fingers into her palms. "Steven—"

"Shh." He kissed her again, and this time when their lips

met, there was a deep, tangible emotion behind the gesture. One that there was no running from, or avoiding.

Moaning, he pressed closer, and cupped her face. The flowers fell to the sidewalk, bouncing between their feet, but they didn't stop kissing. She strained to get closer, and her hands roamed his body, learning everything with new vision. Memorizing every hard edge and muscle. And it wasn't enough.

She needed him *now*.

And it seemed like he had the same opinion, too. He spun her around the corner of her shop, into the dark alley. The second they were cloaked in darkness, he undid her shorts, yanking them down. She gasped and reached for his buckle, unfastening it and ripping his pants open. They didn't waste time with foreplay or soft caresses.

There wasn't any time.

The need was too strong, too loud, to be denied.

Hauling her up against the brick wall, he positioned himself at her entry. He was seconds from sending her soaring into an orgasm, but he stopped. "Shit."

"What?" she asked breathlessly. "Why'd you stop? Don't *stop*."

"I didn't bring a condom. We were supposed to go to a sweet date, like normal people, and fuck at home in a bed… again, like normal people."

Home. He'd called her place home. A strangled laugh escaped her. "We're not normal, and I'm on the pill, so *come on*."

"But…" Still, he hesitated. "Are you sure? I mean, I'm clean, but that's a big step. I've never even fucked without a condom before."

"Yes, I'm sure." She grabbed either side of his face and squeezed. "I'm yours, and only yours. I'm not sleeping with anyone else, and don't want to. And if you don't fuck me right now, I'll kill you."

Something lit his expression—possession, maybe?— and he growled, caught her mouth, and drove inside of her with one hot, hard, long stroke. Unable to bite it back, she screamed into his mouth, and he muffled her cries, pressing even closer to her. He palmed her ass, lifted her a little higher, and slammed into her again.

Her nails scraped over his shoulders, seeking skin to dig into, but he still wore his suit jacket. And for some reason, that made what they were doing even hotter.

Every nerve inside of her bunched in her stomach, tightening more and more with each thrust, and it was only a matter of seconds until she lost it.

And the amazing thing was...

He was just as out of control as she was. He was open, and wild, and raw, and he was *hers*. He broke the kiss off, his breathing ragged. "Jesus, Lauren. Your pussy is so tight and wet and I can't...fuck."

Shaking his head, he caught her mouth again, his movements more frantic. She was right there with him, straining to grasp that orgasm only he could give her. "*Steven*," she cried out, stars bursting in front of her eyes as her orgasm took over her.

Groaning, he thrust into her three more times, and he came, too.

He collapsed, trapping her in between his hard body and the brick wall. After a few ragged breaths, he pulled back enough to look her in the eyes, cupped her cheek, and kissed her forehead. "Shit. That was—real. And you mean more to me than you'll ever fully comprehend. More than I ever thought possible."

Her lids drifted shut. This was what she had been waiting for her whole life. The thing—no, the *man*—she waited for. And she wasn't scared anymore. The truth was, she wasn't even sure why she'd been scared in the first place.

And she was ready to tell him how she felt about him.

No more secrets. No more fear.

"Steven, I—"

"Lauren?" Holt called out, knocking on the door of her bakery. "Are you here? Are you okay? I saw your car out front."

Steven stiffened and whispered, "Shit. Why is he here, looking for you?"

"I…" Her heart skipped a beat. "I'm not sure."

"Get rid of him. I'll wait back here. I don't want him to see me and want to hang out. I want you to myself tonight." He dropped a big kiss on her lips and helped her to her feet. "I don't want to share you with anyone."

"The feeling is mutual." Lauren pulled her shorts up. "I'm back here, tossing a garbage bag in the dumpster. Give me a second."

After hastily dressing, she smoothed her hair and walked around the corner with shaky legs. Steven smacked her butt as she walked by him, grinning happily.

Holt took one look at her and crossed his arms. "You okay?"

Okay. Yeah. She'd roll with that.

Letting out a big yawn, she nodded and covered her mouth. "I am. But I'm about to head home for some rest, so—"

"Is Steven still staying with you?"

She nodded. "Yeah. But I'm really tired and—"

"Okay, I'll be quick. I just stopped by on my way home to thank you for taking care of him. For coming up with a reason—whatever it was—to get him to stay with you. It probably wasn't easy for you to lie to him like that."

Shaking her head, she held a hand up, horror holding her still and mute. In all this happiness and love, she'd forgotten about the one thing that could ruin it all: her lie. But it was all about to come rushing back. Holt was saying all these things, and Steven was behind her, and he was going to ruin everything. "Holt, stop. I didn't—"

"Don't be modest. He cares about you a lot more than he'd ever admit. It's why you needed to be the one to babysit him." Holt grasped her shoulder and squeezed. "If you hadn't lied and come up with a reason to get him to stay, I think—"

"Please shut up!" This was it. This was the moment where it was all going to fall apart. She couldn't stop Holt from speaking. He wasn't *listening* to her. "I didn't—"

"Yeah, you did. And I think your little lie saved…his…life." The last word finished on a whisper, and Holt paled.

Without looking, she knew why he looked like he saw a ghost.

Steven. Watching them. Listening. Learning. Hearing it all.

Holt shifted on his feet. "Steven…hey, buddy. I, uh, didn't see you there."

"Steven." She fisted her hands and faced him. His expression was icy and closed off. "We can explain."

Steven ignored her and addressed Holt. "Can you, now?"

His voice…*God, his voice.* It sounded dead. Unemotional. And just like that?

She remembered why she'd been so scared to let him in. Why she'd been terrified to love him, and need him, and want him. If she lost him…

It would *kill* her.

Chapter Sixteen

That aching, wrenching, painful feeling that echoed like a gunshot in his chest? The one that hurt more than a real fucking bullet ripping through flesh?

Yeah, that was his heart.

And he wasn't a cardiologist or anything, but he was pretty damn sure Lauren had just broken it. It was breaking and cracking and dying, because this whole thing? Lauren kissing him, making love to him, inviting him into her bed and her heart while pretending to want more with him? Yeah, that's all it was. *Pretend*.

All those soft words and whispered promises had all been a lie to keep him at her side, concocted by her and Holt, and he'd fallen for every single word.

And the thing that made this whole thing worse? Even with the proof right there in front of him, screaming at the top of its lungs with bright neon lights, he didn't want to believe it. Didn't want it to be true. An inner voice insisted it wasn't, that it couldn't be, but that voice was fucking insane.

While he was busily picturing a future with her, and two

adorable kids, and a happy life he'd all but given up on...she'd been lying to him. Just like everyone else. That was the worst part. He'd thought she was different. That he could trust her.

That she understood how *important* honesty was to him.

He'd clearly been wrong.

Holding his arms out, he walked out under the streetlights. "Don't stop on my account. I'd love to hear more about your elaborate scheme to keep an eye on me."

Holt shifted on his feet and pushed his glasses into place.

Lauren just stared at him like he was a ghost.

"Well?" Steven asked, laughing. It physically hurt to do so, but it was better than shouting, like he was two seconds from doing. "What lies did you tell me, Lauren? Can you be more specific? Was it the break-in? The things you said that night? Hell, *tonight?*"

She snapped out of whatever trance she'd been in. Stepping forward, she held her hands in front of her in a pleading gesture. "Steven, no. I didn't—"

Steven growled.

Holt grabbed her arm and pulled her back. "Don't."

"Get your hands off of her," Steven said through clenched teeth. "And give me one good fucking reason why I shouldn't kill you, right now, for going behind my back. For making Lauren *babysit* me. For the lies, and the games, and the—"

"Enough. We get it. You're pissed. And you have every right to be." Holt stepped closer, pointing a finger at him. "And the whole babysitting thing? Yeah. That was an unfortunate choice of words. But—"

"You think?" Steven asked, keeping his voice as neutral as he could manage.

Which wasn't very neutral at all.

"I—" Lauren started.

Holt shot her a glance. "I'm sorry. But me and Lydia were worried about you, and the only person we could think of who could help us make sure you were okay was…" Holt stared at Lauren, not finishing his sentence. He didn't need to.

Lauren closed her eyes and her lips moved soundlessly, like she was talking to herself. "I'm sorry," she whispered.

"Go away." Steven clenched his fists. "Leave us."

Lauren's eyes flew open. "O-Okay."

"Not you," he snapped. Glaring at Holt, he jabbed a finger toward him. "You. Go. Now."

Holt hesitated. "You can be pissed at me all you want, but I was worried about you. So I asked Lauren—"

"Yeah. I got that part, loud and clear." Steven ground his teeth together, trying his damnedest not to break. Not now. Not in front of Holt. Not even in front of Lauren. "Now go."

Holt nodded. "Lauren…?"

"It's fine. I'm fine," she said, hugging herself. She seemed anything but *fine*, which perversely made him happy because he wasn't either. "Go ahead."

Holt walked past her, but stopped in front of Steven. "Be pissed at me all you want, but she cares about you. Don't ruin this out of anger."

Steven clenched his fists even tighter and didn't answer.

This—whatever *this* was—was already ruined.

As soon as Holt walked away, and was gone, Lauren stepped forward. "Please, let me explain."

Her pale skin was at stark contrast with the darkness surrounding them, and her blue eyes were full of so many emotions it was like a tornado of feelings. He shut all that out, though. Couldn't afford to feel it. To feel anything.

"There's really not much to explain." He flexed his jaw. "Did you lie to me?"

She flinched. "Y-Yes. But—"

"No. No *buts*. You fucking lied."

"Please, I—" She grabbed his arm. He shook her off. She paled even more and tears spilled out onto her cheeks, but he didn't care. He couldn't. "*Steven.*"

She'd said his name a million times, in lots of different ways. But she'd never said it like this, with pain laced through it. It did things to him. Bad things. When she was in pain, he made it better. Hugged her. Soothed her. But this time, she was in pain because of him, and he was in pain, too.

And he wasn't sure what to do about that.

"You know how much I hate liars," he ground his teeth together, "and you lied to me anyway. Didn't take a chance, out of the million chances you've had, to come clean."

"It wasn't a lie." She shook her head, her cheeks wet. "Not really. Brian did break in, and I was scared…at first."

He growled under his breath. Just moments before, he'd been buried inside of her and had been so sure he was on top of the world. And now…this. "If it wasn't a lie, and it wasn't a big deal, why not tell me? Why hide it and pretend like Holt never asked you to keep an eye on me, or pretend like you were scared at all? Why not just tell me the truth all along?"

She stared at him, opening her mouth and closing it.

No sound came out.

He laughed. "Yeah. Exactly. It was a lie, and you kept it to yourself, knowing how I would feel afterward. That was your choice. And it doesn't even matter that it's a small lie. What matters is that you knew it would upset me, and you did it anyway. And that's what I can't forgive."

He clenched his jaw, all the other times a lie had hurt him coming back to haunt him, but one in particular wouldn't shut up. The time he'd lost all his men. After that, he swore to never let a lie go unquestioned again. To never forgive. Never forget. And he couldn't change that for Lauren. He'd lost too much. Seen too much.

A lie was a lie, no matter how big or small.

She shook her head. "No. Don't say that. I was worried about you, and did what I had to do to keep you with me. Is that so bad?"

"Since you lied about it?" He dragged his hand through his hair. "Yes. It's that bad. You *lied* to me. You know how important honesty is to me, but you smiled and lied more. This whole thing was a way to keep me by your side, and nothing more."

"*No*. It was real." Her lower lip trembled, and she bit down on it. "It was all real."

"The funny thing about lies? They break trust." He let out a short laugh. "I don't fucking believe you anymore."

"What was I supposed to say?" she cried. "That I was worried you might be drinking yourself into a grave? That I asked you to stay with me because you might hurt yourself? That I couldn't bear the thought of you doing anything to harm yourself, so I did the one thing guaranteed to make you hate me? That it was worth the risk?"

He staggered back. "I would *never* do anything like that. If you think I would, you don't know me at all. You never did."

She lowered her lashes, tears streaming down her ghostly pale cheeks. "I was worried about you. I…*I love you*. And I—"

"Don't." The word came out strained. Weak. And that pissed him off. "Don't even think about using that against me. Not now." That came out a hell of a lot stronger.

Good. He needed strength to do what came next.

She bit down on her lower lip even harder to stop it from trembling. It didn't work. "If you don't believe anything else, you have to believe that, at least. Hate me. Love me. Do what you want, but I love you. And I won't stop."

Something pierced through him. It seemed so real, so *there*, that he actually glanced down to see what it was. There was, of course, nothing there. What he felt was the loss of what might have been. The loss of her. "We're done."

"No. No, no, no." She doubled over and pressed a hand to her heart. Did she feel the same penetrating pain he did?

"Don't say that."

He swallowed hard. She was looking at him like he ripped her heart out and stomped on it. And maybe he did. But that was only fair. She'd done it to him, too. She'd taken the one person in this world he trusted—the one person who he thought he could count on to be real with him—and ripped her out of his arms.

There was no coming back from that.

She was no better than the superior officer who lied to him.

"You're just like him."

She shifted on her feet. "Like who? Holt?"

"No. He lied and my men—" He stalked toward her, but forced himself to stop. If he touched her, he wasn't sure what would happen. And he was done talking about what happened to him. Done opening up to her, when she clearly didn't care. "You know what? I'm done here. Good-bye, Lauren."

She shook her head. "*Steven*."

"The last time I lost everything because of a lie, I swore to never forgive"—he pointed at her—"a liar. That's you. I know you don't get it, and you probably think I'm being harsh. But there are some lines I can't cross anymore. For my sanity, so that I can get through the next day—trusting the people I have in my life—that's what is most important. And I stand by that promise I made."

"I'm *sorry*." When he tried to walk past her, she threw herself in his arms and hugged him, holding on tight. "I refuse to let you go. I'm sorry, and I shouldn't have lied, but I love you. Don't push me away. Don't do this."

He ached to wrap his arms around her and hug her close. Tell her he forgave her, that he would forgive her for anything. But he didn't, because he didn't.

He shouldn't be so surprised it was ending like this. He knew deep down, all along, that he didn't deserve a happy ending. It was fitting he wasn't getting one.

Gripping her shoulders, he tugged her off and set her down, at arm's length. "Don't follow me. Don't call me. Just leave me the hell alone."

Then he stormed past her.

She let him this time.

"You promised," she called out, her voice laced with pain—that *he* caused her. He didn't have a fucking clue what to do with that yet. With *any* of this. "You promised you'd never leave me."

He stiffened, his fists clenched tight, and his jaw even tighter. "And you promised you wouldn't lie to me." He took another step. "Guess we're even."

A small, broken sound escaped her. "If you leave now, if you walk away from me, I…I won't let you back in. I won't forgive you. This was the one thing I was scared of, and you promised you wouldn't let it happen. I trusted you. So if you do this…" She choked on a sob. "I'll never forgive you. Only walk away if you're ready to accept that."

Shaking his head, he swallowed hard. His brain was at war with his heart. Lying was his one thing that would break them apart, and *she* knew it. She'd done it anyway.

He could, too.

So he walked away before he did something stupid.

Walked right over the flowers he'd given her, crushing the red petals into the pavement. Lauren sobbed behind him, but he didn't look at her. Didn't stop.

He *couldn't*.

The whole way back to his place, he went over the fight. He replayed it in his head, again and again, until it became scratched and sketchy, like an overplayed record. And he still felt like shit. Still wanted to scream and punch things.

Still wanted to go back and tell her he was sorry.

But what the hell was *he* sorry for?

He got that she was worried about him. He did. But all along, he'd been very clear that honesty in a relationship was the only thing he required. And she'd ignored that.

He didn't know how to accept that, or move on.

Or if he even *could*.

He stopped in front of the bar he'd been in the night he and Lauren first hooked up. The night she called him and begged him to come to her place. She'd been upset, and he could obviously tell something was up. He just hadn't thought she would lie to him like that. Had never suspected that.

Flexing his jaw, he ripped the door open and stumbled inside. He hadn't had a drink in almost a week. No time like the present to make up for lost opportunities.

We were worried about you. You were drinking yourself into a grave.

Yeah, well, watch him do exactly that.

Settling down at the bar, he pulled his wallet out of his pants and opened it.

The bartender—a pretty little blonde—came over, interest clearly written all over her face. She was wasting her time. "What can I do for you?"

"I'll take a double shot of Scotch, and another." He tossed forty dollars on the bar. "Keep them coming till I look like I don't need any more."

She took the money and shoved it in her bra, frowning. "Let me guess. A woman…or a man?"

He didn't answer.

"Yep." She shook her head. "Definitely a woman."

He watched her walk off, hips swinging, and felt nothing. Nothing toward *her*, anyway. Now, toward Lauren? He felt it all. Grief. Pain. Anger. Betrayal.

His phone buzzed. He pulled it out. It was a call. He didn't answer it. Lydia would have to wait to find out if he was all right. He wasn't even sure yet.

The bartender slid a glass toward him. "I went right for the triple."

"Thanks."

She smiled and flipped her hair over her shoulder. "Need anything else?"

His phone buzzed again. "No. I'm fine," he answered, glancing at his screen. It was a text from Lydia. Of fucking course it was.

Are you okay?

He didn't want to answer her, but she was his sister. And he couldn't ignore her. She deserved better.

I'm fine.

A moment, and then:

Holt's worried about you. So am I.

Screw him. He loved Holt, he did. But the man pressed on his last nerve, and he didn't give a damn how he felt right now.

I'm fine. And don't get me started on Holt.

He loves you.

Steven snorted. *He has a stupid way of showing it.*

Is Lauren with you?

He gripped the phone tighter. *No.*

Steve…

Picking up his drink, he frowned at it. He didn't drink it, though.

No. I'm not discussing it with you.

Funny, you didn't listen when I told you the same thing with Holt.

He swallowed and set it down untouched. *I can't.*

Want to come stay with us?

He tugged on his tie and sighed. *No. I'm fine.*

That's the one word that never actually means its meaning.

It was true, and he wasn't. *I'll be fine. I just need time.*

I'm here if you need me.

He set his phone down and picked up his drink again. His phone buzzed again, but he didn't look. Didn't want to talk to anyone or anything—

"You look like you could use some company," some brunette said, sitting down beside him. "Are you all right?"

He didn't want company. And he wasn't all right. But she didn't look the type to get the message. He set down his still full glass for the second time. "No. I'm not in a good mood."

"That's okay. Neither am I. What's your story?"

He spun his drink in a loose circle, shrugged, and didn't pick it up. "My girlfriend broke my heart today."

"Same here," the brunette chick said. "And she walked away afterward."

Ah. So she wasn't going to expect him to go home with her. Good. Steven glared down at his phone. Lauren had texted him. "I'm the one who walked away."

"How did that make you feel?" the woman asked, resting her hand on his arm.

He pushed his full glass away. He didn't want it. Didn't want to drink himself into oblivion. The pain was his, and Lauren's, and he needed to feel it. Just like she was.

"Nothing. Nothing at all."

Chapter Seventeen

Three nights.

That's how long it had been since Steven found out she tricked him into staying at her place. Three days since she'd talked to him, or seen him, or even smelled him. He asked her to leave him alone...so she had. She only sent one text to him, that night, and that was it. It had been simple and short.

I'm sorry.

He never even read it.

On her way home that night, she saw him. He sat at a bar, with a glass of whiskey in front of him, and a pretty brunette on his side, chatting him up. When the brunette placed her hand on his arm, and he didn't shake her off, Lauren's heart shattered even more. She walked away after that. She didn't need to see what came next.

Not even thirty minutes, and he'd moved on already.

That's how much she meant to him.

All along, she knew how this would more than likely end.

He would forget about her, and she would be left to mourn the loss of not only his touch, but also his friendship.

While he was *fine*.

She never should have let him in.

She stirred the icing, taking her anger out on it. Those first two nights, she cried herself to sleep. After doing the same last night, she refused to do it again. She shed enough tears over him, and what she thought he meant to her. It was over. They were over.

It was time to move on, since he clearly had.

The bell over the door jingled. She called out, "I'll be right out."

No one answered.

"Hello?"

Goose bumps rose on her flesh, and she froze.

If it was him…

Setting the spoon down, she walked out into the shop area. The second she rounded the corner, she let out a breath of, well…something. It wasn't Steven. She wasn't sure whether to be relieved, upset, or happy. Everything was all tangled up inside of her in a tight, knotted, unrecognizable ball. "Oh. Hey."

Holt rested his hands on the counter. "How are you doing?"

"Great. I'm great." She dried her hands off with a rag and forced a smile. "You?"

"You haven't been answering Lydia's calls," he said, ignoring her question.

Lauren set the rag down. "I just needed time."

"That's what Steven said."

It was on the tip of her tongue to ask if Holt had seen Steven. If they'd spoken, or if he was okay, but she wouldn't. He cut her off. Forgot about her. She needed to do the same. "How is Lydia, by the way?"

"Good. She wants some pie."

Lauren cocked her head. "I heard you make an excellent one. Why come to me?"

"I didn't have time to bake. The boss kept us late at work." He pointed out the window. Mark was out there, and so was Cooper Shillings. Steven was *not*. "So I figured I would stop in and grab some here on my way home."

Lauren craned her neck to look to the side of the other men.

Holt cleared his throat. "He's not out there. He went home after work."

Of course he did. He wouldn't want to risk seeing her. "Apple pie?"

"Yes, please." Holt pulled his wallet out and frowned. "I'm sorry it went down like that. I never meant to ruin what you two had. We were just making sure he was okay."

"So was I, and we can't regret that."

Holt took the cash in his brown leather wallet. It had a TARDIS on it. "I guess not. He's still barely talking to me, but I can tell he misses you."

"I didn't ask."

"You didn't need to," Holt said kindly.

Nodding, she boxed up the pie and blinked rapidly. No. More. Crying. "That'll be six dollars."

He tossed a ten down. "Keep the change."

"This isn't a tipping establishment."

He shrugged and picked up the box. "Call Lydia back. She's worried about you."

And he walked out. The second the door closed behind him, he walked over to the two other men. Mark glanced in, waved, and smiled. Lauren forced a smile and waved back. They walked away, and she covered her face, sagging against the wall.

It was over. It was actually over.

Shaking herself off, she pushed off the wall. The door opened again, and Mark came in. "Hey, Lauren."

"H-Hi," she said, smiling. "Can I get you something?"

"Do you have any cookies? Like, big, girly, kid-like ones?"

She blinked at him. "Yeah, over there."

He walked over and bent down, staring into the glass case. "I'll take the tiara."

"Okay…"

He glanced up, grinning. "You're confused."

"Hey, if you like tiara cookies, I've got no issue with that."

"It's for my daughter. She's two."

Lauren's jaw dropped. Out of all the things she expected Mark to say, that was pretty much the last thing on the list, underneath *I'm pregnant.* "You have a daughter?"

"Yeah." He pulled cash out. "She loves princesses."

"What little girl doesn't? Who's her favorite?"

He smiled, and his entire face lit up with happiness. "Elsa. Of course. She makes me sing her 'Let It Go' every night."

"Wow." A small laugh escaped her. She couldn't help it. "I had no idea you had a kid."

"Most people don't." He shrugged. "It's not really something I talk about a lot."

He had been set up on a blind date with her, so obviously he wasn't still married. But she was curious. "And your wife…?"

"Is dead." The smile left his face. And what was left behind pulled at her heartstrings. "It's just the two of us now."

"Oh. I'm so sorry for your loss." She folded the bag over and handed it to him. "You can just have it. She sounds delightful."

He shook his head and threw down two dollars. "I'll pay. Thanks, Lauren. And, hey, I hope you're doing okay."

Great. So even he knew about the big fight.

"Yeah." She smiled. "I'm fine."

"Life's too short to pretend to be fine when you're not." He picked up the bag and backed up toward the door. "If it makes you feel any better, he looks worse."

With that, he winked at her and left.

The door closed behind him, and she shook her head. It was an hour till closing, but she was done. She needed to go home, and be alone. The bell rang again, and she forced a smile. "Can I help—? Oh, hey."

Daisy smiled back at her. "I was walking by and smelled apple pie. Did you just make some?"

Lauren laughed, walked to the door, flipped the sign to say closed, and locked the door. "I did, and lucky for you, I was just about to close early. Want to share a piece?"

"Heck yeah," Daisy said, dusting her hands off and coming around the counter. She was petite and redheaded and too gorgeous for words. And *single* for the same reason as Mark. They would be *adorable* together.

Maybe it was the fact that her own life was a freaking wreck, but seeing the two of them happy…maybe together… would make her feel a lot better. "I met someone."

"Already?" Daisy asked, clearly taken aback. "You and Steven just—"

Lauren held a hand up. "God, not for me. For you."

"Not even talking about it." She shook her head. "Not yet. Maybe another day."

"Too soon?" Lauren asked sympathetically. Daisy had lost her boyfriend to a car wreck a year ago. They had been in love, and happy, but that's why she and Mark made sense. They'd both loved and lost and would understand what the other went through. "It's been a year…"

"Way too soon." She crossed her arms. "Let's talk about something else. Anything else besides boys. Please."

Lauren cut into the pie, and nodded. "How's work?"

"Long. Boring." Daisy was a cop. She might look small

and helpless, but she was kick-ass. "No one's robbing anyone or causing trouble. It's been quiet."

"Poor you." Laughing, Lauren slid a plate over. "You're ridiculous."

Daisy laughed, too. "Whatever."

The rest of their conversation focused on work, and life. Anything but love, and broken hearts, and it was great. By the time Lauren left the bakery, she'd made tentative dinner plans for the next day with Daisy, and she felt a little more alive. A little more whole, too.

She'd survive this. Whatever didn't kill you made you stronger.

Even Kelly Clarkson agreed.

She trudged down the sidewalk, hugging her purse to her chest, and tried not to think about him. Tried not to ruin her happy little buzz. So when she pushed her door open, she froze in shock. Either her mind was playing tricks on her and she had gone completely crazy...

Or Steven had just come out of her bedroom.

She gripped the doorknob. "Uh..."

He froze midstride.

Mark was right. He looked awful. His cheekbones were gaunt and his skin was an ashen green. He had huge dark circles under his eyes, like he hadn't slept since he walked out of her life without looking back. He also appeared to be hungover.

Neither of them spoke.

After a while, he tugged on his hair and cleared his throat. "I was getting my stuff out of your place and trying to come up with a good speech for when you got home. I thought you wouldn't be home for another hour or so."

"I left early," she replied, keeping her voice as flat and even as his.

"Yeah, I guessed as much," he answered, hugging his

balled up clothes to his chest. His gaze dipped down her body, leaving a blazing trail of heat in its wake, and her heart sped up. "You look…good."

"You don't."

He laughed. "I haven't been drinking, if that's what you're thinking. Haven't had a drop since the night we got together."

Relief fluttered through her chest. He might be done with her and able to walk away without a second thought, but she still cared about him very much—and if she'd managed to get him to see straight in the process of losing him…at least she had that. "Good."

"I just can't sleep," he admitted.

They fell silent again.

She stared at him.

For the second time, he broke the silence. "Fuck, this is harder than I thought it would be." He rocked back on his heels and let out a small laugh. "Have you seen my blue shirt? I couldn't find it."

She set her bag down and walked past him. Walking over to the bed, she yanked the covers back and pulled out his blue T-shirt. Though she would never admit it to him, she'd slept with it for the past three nights.

Walking back into the living room, she tossed it at him. "Here."

"Oh." He caught it easily enough, even though his arms were already full of clothes. That annoyed her. Everything about him annoyed her, at this point in time. "Thanks."

She didn't reply. This whole thing was ridiculous, and painful, and it just needed to be over. He was treating her like she was a stranger, and she was letting him.

"I guess that's everything."

"Great," she said, sugar sweetly. In her head, she gouged his eyes out. "Bye."

He flinched. "Look, I—"

"Screw off," she snapped. "And get out."

"Why are *you* mad at *me*?" His nostrils flared and he stepped closer, gripping his bundle even tighter. At least he didn't look dead anymore. "I'm not the one who lied."

"Get over it," she snapped, shoving him backward. "And while you're at it, get out, too."

"Shit. I didn't mean to say that." He squared his jaw. "I've been trying to think of what to say to you all damn day, and that wasn't it."

"Then say nothing at all. Just go."

He hesitated. "Lauren, I—"

"No. I don't want to hear it. You're mad I lied? Well, fine. Be mad. See if I care. But I lied because I loved you, and you took that and turned it into some horrible, monstrous thing. And that makes *you* the bad person, not me." She poked him in the chest. "You left me." She poked him again. "You walked away." Again. "And you're the one who decided to be done with us." Backing off, she shook her head. "You're the one who's okay. I'm *not*."

"Okay?" He laughed and dropped his clothes to the floor. He advanced on her, and she stumbled back a step before she forced herself to stand still. "What part of this makes you think I'm okay?"

"You left me. Told me you were done with me." She lifted her chin. "And you're obviously okay with that."

He flexed his jaw and took a step toward her. "I wasn't kidding earlier. I can't sleep."

"Me either."

Another step. One more, and he'd be holding her in his arms, and she couldn't let that happen. Couldn't fall back into his arms. "I can't breathe without you there. I mean, I can, but it's not the same. So, yeah, I can't fucking breathe."

"Me either."

He closed the distance between them. They were toe to

toe, and it would be so easy to give in. To let him kiss her and make her feel better. "I miss you."

"I miss you, too. So much." She held her hand up, placing it on his chest, to keep him from coming any closer. "And you see, that's what makes this whole thing so much harder. I loved you, and I let you in. I really, truly, loved you. And you didn't see that, or care, and you left…just like everyone else."

Something inside of him seemed to break. He covered her hand with his, his face ravaged. "Shit. I've been trying to come up with a way to truly express how much I regret walking away that night. I was upset. I was an idiot. But I didn't mean to hurt you. I would never intentionally do that to you."

"Well, you did. You asked me to ignore all my fears and let you in, and swore you wouldn't hurt me, or leave me. You promised me." She swallowed hard and tears trailed down her cheeks. So much for her vow to stop crying over him. "And then you did both of those things in one night. You ruined everything, and you ruined me. I hate you for that. I love you, but God, I hate you, too. So much."

He shook his head, his hands in tight fists at his sides. "No. You can't hate me."

"Yeah, I can."

He stared at her, not speaking.

"Go on. Walk away again." She stepped away from him and hugged herself. "It's what you're good at, right? Show me one last time."

"Lauren—I fucked up." He shoved a hand through his hair and locked eyes with her. What was hidden there— desperation and pain—echoed within her soul. "When I found out you lied, I just—"

She swallowed. "Ran. You ran."

"Yeah." He dropped his hand back to his side and curled his fingers into a ball. "I'm a fucking idiot."

She held on to her elbows tightly. It was the only way she'd be able to stop herself from reaching out and grabbing him—and never letting go. But after he hurt her, left her, ruined her...she wouldn't. She wouldn't fall fast, and hard, like she had last time.

Never again.

All those years, she'd been right to hold her heart close.

"Good-bye, Steven."

"I'm sorry, Lauren," he rasped, his eyes threatening to pull her into their stormy hazel depths. "So damn sorry."

Closing her lids, closing *him* out, she shook her head. He was a rabbit hole, and she was Alice, but she wouldn't fall down again. "You need to go."

He didn't move.

Neither did she.

Finally, she sensed him bend down and pick up his stuff. He walked toward the door, but stopped in front of her. He ran his thumb over her jaw and bent down, kissing her forehead. "I'll go, but I'm going to fix this."

Her heart twisted and turned, and it took all her control not to open her eyes. Not to lean in and wait for another kiss. "There's nothing left to fix."

"Oh, cupcake." His fingers tightened on her. "You're so damn wrong."

And then he left.

She collapsed against the wall, breathing heavily, and still didn't look. She didn't want to see the absence of him, because God, she could already feel it. His missing clothes, and shoes, and the book he'd left on her coffee table the other night. That would be gone, too. It would all be missing. She was empty.

Everything was empty.

Chapter Eighteen

The next afternoon, Steven closed his computer and scratched his head, staring at the clock. In one minute, it would be five o'clock. That meant in that little amount of time, he could go to Lauren's bakery. Ever since she'd asked him to leave yesterday, he'd been brainstorming ways to show her he wouldn't walk out on her...*again*.

Leaving had been the stupidest thing he ever did.

And in his life, he had done a lot of fucked up shit.

His door opened, and he glanced up. His boss, Cooper, stood there, wearing a dark gray suit and an even darker frown. "Have you seen the Yarros file?"

Steven's latest assignment. It had been a damn snoozefest of a case. All the old man did was play golf, drink coffee, and watch *Wheel of Fortune*.

Thank God the gig was over.

"Yeah, I have it." He picked up the tan folder and walked it over to Cooper. "Here you go. All signed off and closed. He's on a plane back to Europe."

His brown-haired, green-eyed boss took it, smiling.

"Great, thanks."

"No problem."

Cooper rifled through it, and slammed it shut. "Your next assignment will be in conjunction with Mark. The new guy."

Shit. The dude was nice. A good worker, even. But the fact that Lydia had set Lauren up with him, and Lauren had seemed to *like* him, made Steven *not* like him.

And there was no changing that.

"Great."

Cooper tilted his head. "You have a problem with him?"

"No, of course not. He's a good guy."

"Yeah, he is." Cooper frowned. "More than you know. Be nice to him."

"I'm always nice."

Cooper smirked. "Unless it's something to do with Lauren. I heard you fucked that up pretty bad. Want some advice?"

Well, shit. The last thing he needed was someone else telling him how much of an idiot he was. He'd told himself that enough. "The Shillings love doctor strikes again? Thanks, but no thanks. I don't need any help."

The man might be his boss, but more than that, he was a friend. A friend who had no right sticking his nose in Steven's business. Cooper had a reputation of trying to help his employees when they, inevitably, messed things up with their woman.

But that didn't mean the help was welcome.

It wasn't.

Cooper shrugged. "If you guys would stop fucking up all the time, I wouldn't have to play the part."

"I'm working on fixing that," he growled. "On my own."

Cooper nodded. "Good. Then you don't need my help."

"Nope."

"All right." He opened the door before giving it anyway.

"Just remember. Grand gestures, and professions of love, never fail. Women forgive us, if the heart is there."

Yeah. He wasn't so sure Lauren would forgive him, but he would find a way to make it happen, or he would spend the rest of his life trying. "Thanks, boss."

Cooper nodded and left.

Steven followed him, walking past Holt's office. The door was cracked open, and Lydia sat in the chair in front of his desk, grinning. Holt looked happy as a pig in shit. He held a small square piece of paper. "I can't fucking believe it. This is her?"

Lydia laughed. "Or him."

Unable to resist, Steven knocked on the half-opened door.

Lydia jumped to her feet, the smile fading. "Steven—"

"I'm—" Holt started, shoving the paper out of view.

"Don't. I just popped in to tell you I forgive you for the lie. Your heart was in the right place, and so was Lauren's. If I didn't trash everything completely, I'll do everything I can to get her to come back to me. I'm going to fix it."

Lydia pressed a hand to her stomach. "Do you need help?"

"Go get her," Holt said at the same time, grinning.

"I am. And, no, Lyd. This is something I've gotta do on my own, but thanks. Also, by the way, you two aren't fooling me." He pointed at the paper Holt had hastily hidden under his laptop. "Congratulations. Can't wait to meet her—or him."

Lydia's jaw dropped.

Holt pushed his glasses into place and smiled.

Steven grinned and left them to their moment. It was time to chase after his. He waited impatiently for the elevator, scowling at the closed doors that kept him from his girl. The bakery was walking distance from his work, so he decided to go by foot. The whole way there, he went over the speech he had in his head. He had it all planned out.

And it fucking rocked.

But she was gone. The lights were out, and he was alone on her sidewalk. She closed early. Again. She never did that. Never left work. It soothed her. Gave her a purpose. And he fucked that up for her. All of it. But he would fix it.

Some way, somehow, he would.

He stalked toward her apartment, each stride longer than the last. When he got to her doorstep, he lifted his hand and knocked. After a few minutes, it became apparent she wasn't home. So he sat. And he waited. And waited.

And waited some more.

Her elderly neighbor came, and went, and came again, her arms full with grocery bags. She must've taken pity on him. "She went out with a friend for dinner. She might be home soon."

"Thanks, Mrs. Seechler."

She smiled gently, her soft gray hair in a bun. "You're welcome, Steven. Would you like to come in and wait? I can make tea, and I just bought some fresh baked cookies."

"That's very kind of you," he said gently, forcing a smile. "But I'll wait here. I don't want to risk missing her."

Plus, he deserved to sit on the hard concrete stairs.

He'd known, deep down, when she lied to him about the break-in, that she had done it out of love. There was no doubt in his mind. But his knee-jerk reaction had been to leave. To punish her for hurting him, and in a way, it was an excuse to escape the overwhelming happiness she made him feel. The love she made him feel. Yeah, that's right. He fucking loved her. And it scared the shit outta him.

Guys like him didn't deserve happiness.

So it was only right he lose it, like the rest of his men had.

But his decision to deprive himself of his one chance at a happy ending wasn't fair, and he'd made a mistake in leaving her standing alone, outside her bakery. It wasn't a mistake he would make again.

He could be fucking happy, too.

And he'd spend the rest of his life showing her how.

"If you're sure…" she said.

"I am. But let me help you carry those in."

He set his flowers down and took the bags from her. By the time he left her apartment, he'd declined tea and cookies at least three times. Walking out into the dark night, he sat back down, stretched his legs out…

And waited some more.

By the time familiar footsteps rounded the corner, it was close to nine o'clock. He didn't stand. Just sat there, waiting for her. With flowers.

Like the sorry fool he was.

When she came around the corner, she wasn't alone. She had a friend with her, one he vaguely recognized as someone she hung out with from college. For the life of him, he couldn't remember her name. But he was pretty sure it had something to do with a flower or a plant.

"That's awful," the girl whose name he couldn't remember said. "And he just went home after that?"

"Yep." Lauren dug in her purse. "And, hey, moving on… about that guy you might like."

"Oh, God. Not again."

"But this one's good. His name is Mark, and he works at the Shillings Agency."

Steven gripped the flowers tighter.

Fucking Mark.

"Stop right there." Her friend shook her head. "Prior military?"

"Yeah, but—"

"No way. Those men are way too hesitant to let people in." She glanced at Lauren and flinched. Steven did, too. She was right. "Oops. Sorry."

"It's fine," Lauren said, but her voice was tight. "But this guy's different. He's handsome and sweet and a single—" She broke off, stumbling back a step.

Fuck. He'd finally been spotted.

It was go time.

"Hi," he said, forcing a smile. "You look beautiful, Lauren."

And she did. Then again, he couldn't remember a time when she hadn't been absolutely breathtaking. Even back in elementary school, when he'd spotted her panicking because she didn't have a number two pencil, she'd been stunning.

"Thanks," Lauren muttered.

The other woman glanced up, and scowled. "What are you doing here?"

"Waiting. With flowers." He stood and smoothed his jacket nervously. "Sorry, I didn't realize you wouldn't be alone."

"Have you been here since you left work?" Lauren asked.

"Well, I stopped by the bakery first, but yeah."

Lauren held her keys tightly and hugged her purse to her chest. "That was four hours ago."

"Yep. It was." He swallowed. "I'd have waited four more, too."

"I went to dinner with Daisy," she said, not looking the slightest bit swayed by his statement. "We made plans yesterday."

Ah, yes. Daisy Gallagher. "Nice to see you again, Daisy."

Daisy stared back at him blankly, playing with her red side braid.

"Anyway, it's late. And you've been out here all night, so I think I'm gonna crash." Lauren forced a tight smile. "It was nice seeing you, though."

He shifted on his feet. "We need to talk. I'll wait out here till tomorrow morning, after you get a good night's sleep, if I have to. It's not like I'm actually getting any myself anyway."

Lauren cleared her throat. "Did you need something?"

"Yes." *You.* "I, uh, brought you flowers."

Lauren gaped at Daisy.

Daisy glared back.

Finally, Lauren glanced back his way. "You don't need to do this."

"Yeah, I do. I'm sorry. I miss you. I'm sorry."

Daisy nibbled on her lower lip, watching them with wide green eyes. "Uh…I'm going to go now."

"Don't," Lauren said.

"It was nice seeing you," Steven said at the same time.

Daisy gave him one last look. "I know where you live."

"Duly noted," Steven said drily.

After she walked away, Lauren crossed her arms and tapped her foot. "Stop doing this."

"Doing what?"

"Showing up at my place, trying to apologize. It won't work." She brushed past him, keys in hand, and ignored the flowers. He followed her closely—which she clearly didn't miss. Her shoulders stiffened, and her hand trembled as she slid the key into the lock. "You said we were done, so we're done. Accept it."

He rested a hand on her doorjamb, directly over her head. "That easy?"

"It was for you, wasn't it?"

"No. It wasn't." He gripped her hand. She still hadn't gotten the key in the lock. Gently, he took them from her, slid it in, and turned it. "And it's not that easy for you. If it were, you wouldn't care that I keep showing up. You wouldn't be scared of what I might make you feel."

"I'm not scared of you," she said automatically. "Someone once said only the things worth fighting for scare you."

He flinched. "Turning my own words back on me?"

"If the shoe fits…" She lifted a shoulder and twisted the

knob. When she turned and tried to shut it in his face, he inserted *his* shoe in between the door and the jamb. "*Steven.* Go away."

"You're not scared of me." He rested his head on the wood, watching her from under lowered lids. "Or of what I make you feel?"

"No, of course not," she said quickly, her cheeks flushed a fetching pink.

"Prove it. Let me in for one last game of truth or dare." He held the flowers out, his heart racing. This hadn't been his *plan.* This was impulsive, and out of his control, and not the ideal situation. But it just might work. "If, by the end of it, you still want me to leave, I'll go. No questions asked."

She hesitated. It was in her eyes, and her tight grip on the door, and in the way she watched him, like she was scared he might just prove her wrong. He was damn well planning on doing exactly that. "Why should I even bother, when I can simply refuse to let you in?"

"We've been friends for years. That's a lot to just throw away." He locked gazes with her and refused to let go. If she was going to send him away, and reject his attempts to make things right, she would look him in the eye and do it. "Please, Lauren."

For a second, he thought she might kick his foot out of the way and slam the door in his face. She had every right to. But something he said must have changed her mind. She stepped back and opened the door. "Fine. Come in."

Heartbeat pounding, he shut the door behind him. She headed toward her bedroom and kicked her heels off. She wore a tight red dress that made his mouth water, but he had to focus on the important shit tonight. He had to show her he could treat her right...

If she gave him the chance.

And he wouldn't fuck it up again.

Chapter Nineteen

There was something in Steven's eyes, and his voice, that no matter how hard she tried, Lauren couldn't ignore. The simple words weren't much, just him asking to play a silly game to prove something to her, but the emotion behind them punched her in the chest. Each word, each look, slowly melted away her anger and fear...

Until she found herself opening the door.

But now what was she supposed to do with him?

After she kicked her heels off, she tucked her hair out of her face and turned to him. He watched her with a fiery passion she couldn't ignore. "Do you want a drink? Maybe ten?"

"No," he said, shaking his head. "I told you, I haven't had any since the night we got together. That was the truth."

"Funny, I saw you the night you left me," she said, without really wanting to. It just slipped out. "Chatting it up with some girl, with booze in front of you. It was like I stepped through a time portal and nothing had even happened between us. Like those few days we shared were nothing."

He rubbed his jaw and shook his head. "She sat next to me, not the other way around. And I didn't go home with her, or kiss her, or fuck her. Or even flirt with her."

"I didn't ask."

"You didn't need to," he answered, crossing his arms. "Don't worry, I won't count that as your question."

She leaned on the wall. "Oh, the game started?"

"Didn't it start the second you let me in?" he asked, his voice low.

"No, but it did now." She walked across the room to the couch and perched on the edge of it. "That was a bad first question, but to each his own, I guess."

He grimaced. "Your turn."

"Why are you here?"

He took a few steps closer. "I miss you, and I'm sorry I reacted the way I did. If I had it to do over again I would show you that you can trust me, and I won't run. If you give me another chance, I'll never run again. I promise."

She swallowed hard and let out a laugh. She couldn't help it. "Funny, you already broke one promise to me just a few days ago. But I'm supposed to think they mean something to you now?"

"They do. You do." He stepped closer. "It does."

She averted her face. He was looking at her as if he couldn't live without her, and yet he'd been fine with telling her he was done with her the second she disappointed him. She wasn't sure what to believe. His words or his actions. "Your turn."

"What will it take to get you to forgive me?"

She bit down on her tongue and shook her head. "There's nothing to forgive. You said you were done with me, so I'm letting you be. You said it's over, so it is. I told you if you walked away, not to come back. And you still did it."

"I don't want it to be over."

"The friendship?" she asked, tapping her fingers on her knees. "Or the sex?"

"Both. All of it. What we were only just discovering." He took another step. Every time he answered her, he moved closer. She had three more questions before he would be right there, at her side, within touching distance. "I want it all. All of you. All of me. All of us. The good. The bad. The happiness. The tears. Everything."

When he said things like that…

It made it a lot harder to remember why she shouldn't trust him again.

And it was more difficult to remember the pain he caused when he walked away, and metaphorically brushed her off his hands. It made her aching heart want to trust him again, despite all that. But he needed to be all in. To be as head over heels about her as she was about him.

And that was one thing he hadn't mentioned yet.

Love.

She'd told him she loved him. He'd walked away. And that was that. "Then you should have let me explain."

"I know," he said, his voice low. "Let me tell you about what happened over there. When I lost my men."

She stiffened. "Why now?"

"It plays hand in hand with my reaction." He took a deep breath, locking eyes with her. "The guys I lost? It was all because of a lie. My superior lied to me, and I knew it, and I didn't question him. I let it slide. And men died."

Swallowing, she stepped closer. "Tell me everything."

"I will. This time, I won't leave a damn thing out, either. He called me and told me I had to take my men on a routine raid. There were supposedly weapons left behind in an abandoned house, and we were supposed to retrieve them so the enemy couldn't use them against us. Clear cut and easy."

She bit her lip and nodded. "Go on."

"There was something in his voice, in the way he spoke, that told me he was lying. I sensed it, and I didn't call him on it because he was my superior officer, and it wasn't my place to question orders." He stared at the window, seeming like he was in another time or place. "We got there, and I knew something was off. It was too quiet. Not the empty kind of quiet—the kind that tells you everything is hiding for a reason. Before I could call out a warning, a shot rang out."

She swallowed hard. She didn't want to hear this...but at the same time, she needed to. "Was that when you got shot?"

"No. The first bullet hit my buddy Sam. Right through the throat. He choked on blood and died right next to me, and there was nothing I could do to save him. I tried to stop the blood with my hands." He held out his hands, staring down at them. She had a feeling he didn't see them as clean. In his eyes, they were probably drenched with blood. "Nothing worked. He bled out."

She closed her eyes, forcing the tears to stay back. It was a losing battle and she knew it. "That's horrible. I'm so sorry, Steven."

"One by one, I watched my men get shot, as they yelled out that it was an ambush. I called for backup that didn't come fast enough. Roger got shot in the head, right under his helmet. He died fast a couple yards away from me. Tom took one to the thigh, on his artery, and he passed a lot slower. The rest of the men fell, but I don't know exactly how. I was too busy trying to save them—and failing."

She shook her head. "It's not your fault."

"Then I got shot in the shoulder, and thought I would die, too. All because of a lie I wasn't brave enough to stand up to." He seemed to shake himself off, and he was back with Lauren, in her living room. His eyes were still haunted, though. "And that's when I swore to never forgive another lie. To never forget what those men lost that day, because I was too much of a pussy to call another guy out."

She shook her head. "I'm sorry. So sorry."

"Me too." He cleared his throat and rubbed the back of his neck. "But none of that was your fault, so I shouldn't have acted like you were as guilty as him. In a way, I think I pushed you away because I felt bad for being so happy, when the rest of my men are dead."

She closed her eyes. So much of what he did—how he'd been since coming home—made sense now. "It's not your fault those men died. Their deaths rest at the feet of that superior of yours."

"I disagree." He lifted a shoulder, not meeting her eyes. "My turn to ask a question, I think. Why did you lie to me? What did you hope to gain?"

"That's two questions," she pointed out, heart racing.

"You asked two, too."

Crap. She had. "I didn't want you to find out how worried we were. If you got mad, you'd walk away. And I wouldn't be able to help you." She gave him a pointed look. In the end, he did exactly that. He shuffled his feet. "And I didn't hope to gain anything at all. I was just making sure you were okay. That's it."

"I am okay," he said slowly. "Because of what you did. Instead of acting like you killed my puppy, I should've stayed and listened."

She didn't say anything to that. Really, what was there to say? "What would have happened if you had?"

"I don't know." He lowered his head. "Because I didn't."

"Your turn," she said.

"Do you really hate me?"

Biting down on her lip, she nodded. "Yes, in some ways. But there's been lots of times where I hated you. When you left for war. When you didn't email me. When you kept sleeping with women you didn't care about, while I was right there…"

He took another step. "I was an idiot. I didn't see what was right in front of me. I'm like a Taylor Swift song, come to life."

A small laugh escaped her. She couldn't help it.

"Ah, that sound." He closed his eyes and breathed deep. "I thought I'd never hear it again, and that scared me even more than my feelings for you do. Your laugh makes me think the future isn't so bleak. It gives me hope for a better life. A better world. If you're in it, it's brighter. There's just no escaping that."

Tears blurred her vision, but she blinked them back. "Wow."

"Your turn," he said, his voice somehow deeper. Richer.

"Do you hate me for lying to you?"

He let out a laugh. Short. Brittle. "No. I could never hate you. Not in a million years." He paused and took another step toward her. One more, and their legs would be touching. "I promise."

She laughed again, but this one was forced. "You're just throwing them out there, all over the place now, aren't you?"

"For you? I'll promise it all. The world. The moon. Happiness. Unlimited orgasms. Home cooked meals. Cuddles. A good-night kiss every night. Two kids. A dog. A fence." He held his arms out. "Me. Anything you want, it's yours. I'll promise it to you and find a way to deliver."

Her heart wrenched. He looked at her with so much honesty and emotion burning behind those hazel eyes of his, there was no doubt he was telling the truth.

If she let him in, he would give her the world. All those things she'd only ever dreamed about would be hers. All she had to do was let him in.

Could she?

"Your turn," she breathed.

"You said you loved me. Like, *really* loved me." He curled

his hands into fists at his sides, his chest rising and falling rapidly. "Do you still?"

Oh, no way she was answering that. She'd already told him she loved him, and he hadn't said it back. There was no way she was going to say it again. Not like this. "Dare."

"Fine." His fingers uncurled, flexed, and fisted again. "Kiss me."

"Excuse me?" she asked, her breath coming faster and her pulse racing.

"You heard me. Answer the question..." He stood directly next to her and held his hand out. "Or kiss me. Those are your choices."

Sliding her hand into his, she tried to stand on her own two feet but wobbled. Just the sensation of his skin on hers was enough to send her reeling backward. She missed him. Loved him. Wanted him. But he had to love her, too. She wasn't willing to risk it all on a whim, or a let's-see-how-this-goes. It had to be all or nothing. "Steven..."

"I can handle it. If you don't love me anymore, just say it. It won't send me spiraling into a bottomless hole of despair and booze and women. I'm done with that shit. There's only one woman I want, and she's right in front of me," he said, his voice edgy. "What's it gonna be? A kiss, or the truth? Which one scares you more?"

"And if I choose neither?"

"Then you lose, and I win, and I'm going to kiss you anyway, because, damn it, Lauren, I need to." He ran his hand up and down her back, under her hair, stopping right above her butt. It was gentle, yet somehow possessive, all at once. "I need your lips on mine. Your arms around my neck. Your legs around my waist. Your heart, and mine—"

She launched herself into his arms, refusing to think about it further. If he kept talking like that, she wasn't sure how this whole thing would end. So she did the one thing she could think of to shut him up. She completed her dare. She kissed him. And the second their mouths touched, all of the doubt and worry faded away for the millionth time. That's how it always worked, though. In his arms, with him holding her, she always believed in him. In this. In them.

His hands splayed on her lower back, and he hauled her against his body, his touch possessive and domineering, yet somehow gentle. If she pulled back, if she gave any indication of wanting to end the kiss, he wouldn't fight her. Wouldn't try to change her mind. And there was heady power to that, and to her own willingness to see how far she let him go, that made her feel in control instead of him.

And she suspected he did that on purpose.

Groaning, he pressed even closer, his mouth ravaging hers as he gripped her dress tightly, seconds from ripping it off her. She could let him. Forget about all the things that needed to be said. Pretend it didn't matter, and that they could build a future on this.

But that would be a lie.

And she wasn't a liar.

Breaking the kiss off, she rested her hands on his chest, gasping for air since he stole all hers with his touch and his kiss. And somehow, she managed to keep her wits about her long enough to sound coherent. Or coherent enough, anyway.

"Dare accomplished. My turn. Do I still scare you?" she asked.

He dropped his forehead on hers, letting out a tortured groan. "Cupcake...yes. I see my future in your eyes, and I see myself, too. But the thing that sucks is if you walk away, if you decide I'm not worth the risk? I'll lose it all. Everything that matters to me most would be walking away with you, so, yeah, you scare the living shit out of me."

She gripped his shirt so tightly it hurt. "Steven..."

"And even more, it terrifies me that you mean so much to

me. That you leaving me would kill me. It's a lot of power to give someone, when you hand them your heart. They could crush it. Break it. Tear it in two." He skimmed his hands up her back, over her shoulders, and lifted her chin to his. His touch was gentle yet strong. Firm. Unwavering. "Or they could take it, and show you what the world could really be like, if only you dared to trust them. And that's what you've done to me."

Cautious joy burst through her chest, spreading outward. "I—"

"Wait, let me finish. I need to say this. No matter how this ends, you have my heart. You might not have noticed or even cared, but I gave it to you years ago. My brain was just too slow to catch on till now. I love you, Lauren Brixton. I've loved you my whole life, and I will continue to love you for the rest of my years." He dropped down to his knees, holding onto her hands firmly. "This I swear to you, here and now. It is the most important promise I have ever made, or will ever make. I promise to love you till the day I die. Hell, screw that. I won't stop even then. I promise to love you forever. I'll never stop. Never waver. Never doubt. I love you, Lauren. So damn much it hurts. I only hope you can love me, someday, the same way you did before I broke your heart. Please say you can. That you will." He took a deep breath. "Say you're mine."

She blinked at him, unable to speak or look away. His speech, as impassioned as it was, came straight from the heart. She knew him, and how he liked to plan things. There was no way that was planned, and that only made it all the more special.

So she needed a minute to fully appreciate it.

But apparently she appreciated it too long.

After a while, he tightened his hold on her chin, his jaw flexing, and cleared his throat. "Are you going to say something? I think I'll take anything at this point. Even a comment on the weather would be acceptable. Or last night's game…"

A small laugh escaped her, and she covered her mouth to hold it back. "Ask me again," she said softly, trying her best to keep her voice steady.

"Ask you what aga—?" His expression lit up with knowledge, and something else she couldn't name. Hope, maybe. "Oh. *Oh*. Do you still love me like that?"

"With all my heart, body, and soul." She fisted his shirt and pulled him closer. "Forever and always."

He lowered his face to hers, stopping just short of kissing her. "Is that a promise, cupcake?"

"Oh, yeah. It's totally a promise."

He gave her the most beautiful, pure, bright smile ever to grace the face of this earth, and he kissed her again. This time, his lips lingered on hers, and it went from a way to seal their promise to something a lot more out of control.

It quickly became about getting closer to one another.

Gripping the hem of her dress, he ended the kiss long enough to yank it off, then reclaimed her mouth with a predatory growl. "Mine."

She nodded, undoing his shirt with trembling fingers as he undid her bra with a flick of his wrist. Before she even had his shirt off, she was completely, utterly naked.

"I win," he breathed, grinning.

Then he swung her into his arms, tossing her over his shoulder, and strode into her room. As soon as he got to her bed, he lobbed her down on it. She hadn't even stopped bouncing before he was on her, kissing a path up her inner thigh.

He didn't waste time. Didn't hesitate. Just closed his mouth over her clit and rolled his tongue over her wet, aching flesh. And, God, it felt *good*.

It hadn't been all that long, in all reality, since they'd been together. But for a while there, she had been sure she would never have this again. Never have him.

So it had felt like a lifetime.

He slid his hands under her butt, lifting her higher and holding her tightly. She rolled her hips against his mouth, seeing stars already and she hadn't even come yet. That's how good he was, and that's how *hers* he was. He stroked and strummed her till she was primed and ready to go, and he always delivered.

"Steven," she cried, burying her hands in his hair and holding on for dear life.

He growled and thrust two fingers inside of her, deepening his intimate kiss. That's all it took to throw her over the abyss, and she came so hard her body literally vibrated from it. After he gently lowered her to the mattress, he undid his zipper with less than steady hands, kicked his pants off, and was on her.

"Hold on tight, cupcake." He skimmed his hand up her leg and hauled it against him. He pressed his cock against her clit, slapping it once. "I'm gonna make up for lost time."

That short amount of pressure sent her over the edge all over again. "Oh my — *Steven*."

"Damn right," he growled. He thrust inside of her with one hard, long stroke. "All." A thrust that made her toes curl. "Fucking." Another that made her cry out. "Yours." This time, he reached that spot that most people only ever dreamed about.

And she came again.

He kept moving inside of her, his expression open and vulnerable and so damn sexy it brought tears to her eyes. He held nothing back from her, not anymore. And it was easily the most moving moment she'd ever experienced, watching him as he found his own pleasure. But he wasn't content to leave her there, even though he already made her come too many times to keep track of.

Licking his finger, he reached between them and massaged

her clit, grinning when she tensed beneath him and dragged her nails down his chest. His fingers kept moving, and he kept thrusting inside of her, and impossibly, the pressure inside of her built up again. She couldn't keep track of the words that exploded from her mouth.

Pleas. Curses. Threats. They all came.

There was no controlling herself.

The pressure inside of her built higher, until finally it all just exploded, and euphoria spread through all her limbs. And this time, he was right there with her. He stiffened and came, pressing inside of her one last time before falling on top of her.

Rolling to the side, he dragged her with him, so she lay half across him, and half on the bed. He caught her hand, curling his fingers around it and holding tightly.

"Thank you for giving me a second chance." Lifting it to his mouth, he kissed the back of it, his chest rising and falling in time with hers. "I love you, Lauren. I will always love you. And I'm going to spend the rest of my life loving you more and more every day. I've never been surer of anything."

She smiled and buried her face in his shoulder, inhaling his crisp, manly scent. "I love you, too, and I plan on doing all those things and more. You make me happy. Secure. And that feeling is something I never thought I'd get."

"Well you better get used to it," he said, hugging her closer and kissing her temple. "I'm not going *anywhere*."

"Thank God for that," she murmured, tracing a heart on his chest.

"Despite everything I said, and how angry I got, I was drowning myself in things I shouldn't have been. I was on a downward spiral, and you saved me." He smoothed her hair back from her face, staring at her with an open honesty that made her heart stop. "You saved me, time and time again, and I'll never forget that. I only wish I'd realized I loved you sooner. But I'll make up for the time we lost together. I swear that."

As her lids drifted shut, he continued to gently massage her scalp. There was no doubt in her mind that he meant every word. And that was amazing. Inspiring. Life changing. All this time, she wanted him as hers. She'd just been waiting for him to want those same things. And for whatever reason, he finally had.

He was hers.

And she was never letting go.

Epilogue

"She's so cute, and tiny, and that strawberry blonde hair is adorable," Lauren said, smiling. The moonlight lit up her hair, and she was hauntingly beautiful in the dim lighting. Like usual. "And Rose is such a pretty name. I wonder how they thought of it?"

Steven laughed. He knew exactly where the name originated. "She's a Doctor's companion. Their favorite. If you watched it, you'd know that."

"I wonder if our baby would get your strawberry blond hair," she said, her tone lost in thought as she ignored his comment. "And maybe my eyes."

"I don't have strawberry blond hair. Only girls have it. Like Strawberry Shortcake, and Lydia. Mine's red."

She rolled her eyes. "Okay, honey. Whatever you say."

Laughing, he climbed the stairs. He held their takeout dinner in his arms, and even though it was after ten o'clock at night, they'd just left the hospital. After five hours of labor, Lydia had delivered a healthy baby girl. She and Holt had been so happy, and so in love, that it had been beautiful. When they smiled down at their baby girl, holding her and glowing with happiness, it had hit Steven pretty damn hard.

He wanted that. A baby.

So badly it fucking hurt.

But more than a baby, he longed for a family. One that he and Lauren created together out of love and trust. A week ago, he bought a ring. He'd been waiting for the perfect time to ask her to marry him, but he hadn't found it yet.

Tonight was it.

He was ready.

Unlocking the door, he opened it and tried to smile at her as she passed, though he probably looked deranged. His suspicions proved right. She paused and blinked at him. "Are you all right?"

Widening his smile, he nodded. "Yes, of course."

"I spooked you, didn't I?" She walked past him, shaking her head. "I wasn't saying I was ready to pop out a few kids right now, just for the record."

He set the food down and swallowed hard, patting his suit jacket pocket. It was still there. He shrugged out of it and tossed it across the chair. Without speaking, he walked into their bedroom and retrieved the one thing he needed.

"Do you?" he called out. "Want kids, that is?"

She didn't answer. When he came out of the bedroom, she hadn't moved from where he left her. Her face was pale, and her lips were parted, and she stared down at something between her feet.

The box. With a ring inside of it.

Shit.

"You weren't supposed to see that yet," he said. He curled his fist around the small, circular object he held. "I wasn't ready."

"It fell out of your coat." She bent down and picked it up, pressing her other hand to her heart, which was more than likely racing. He didn't blame her. His was, too. This was a huge fucking step. "Steven…"

"I know. Believe me, I know." He walked over to her, not hesitating in his stride, or his decision. He loved Lauren and was ready to spend the rest of his life with her. This was, in a lot of ways, the easiest, simplest choice he'd ever made. "I love you."

"I love you, too," she said quickly, a little bit more color suffusing her cheeks. "So much."

"I want to marry you." He knelt at her feet, on one knee. "But this isn't a decision I came to quickly. It took me years and years. Hell, I even asked you to marry me years ago. It wasn't a joke, or a backup plan. You have always been my life. My heart. My happiness. And it's time to take the next step. To promise myself to you forever and ever, officially."

Tears ran down her face, and her lip quivered. Hopefully they were those damn happy tears, instead of painful ones. Why were women so fucking hard to read? "Steven…"

"It might seem fast, but we've been best friends for our whole damn lives. I held this very ring up to you at the lake all those years ago." He held out the twist tie between two fingers. She bit down on her lip. Hard. "And I asked you to marry me. Well, I'm asking you again. This time, with a real ring. And a real promise behind it." Setting the old ring down, he took the ring box out of her hand. She didn't want to let go. He had to pry it loose. After popping the lid, he met her eyes and asked, "Lauren Brixton, will you do me the incredible honor of becoming my wife?"

She dropped to her knees and cradled his face, not even glancing at the ring. "I said it on that lake, all those years ago, and I'm saying it now. Yes. God, yes. So much yes."

Laughing, she kissed him. She tasted like tears and heaven and *her*. He'd never grow tired of that. Or of her. She made him better. Happier. Whole. He took over the kiss, capturing her lips under his, and he rolled her onto her back. He lay on top of her, in his favorite place in the world, and pulled back. Smiling, he kissed the tip of her nose. Taking the ring out of the box, he grabbed her hand.

As he slid the ring on her left ring finger, he felt a rush of satisfaction. She was his. And, more importantly, he was hers. "This makes it official."

She wiggled her fingers and smiled at the princess-cut diamond. "I hate to break it to you, but it was official at the lake all those years ago. I was just waiting for you to see it, too."

"Sorry it took me so damn long." He grunted, rolling his hips so his dick pressed against her sweet pussy. "But I'm here now…"

"Yes." She wrapped her legs and arms around him. "And, by the way, my answer to your other question is yes, too."

He skimmed his hand up her thigh, pausing just short of her ass. "What question?"

"Kids. I want them."

His heart skipped a beat, and rushed straight ahead. "You do?"

"I do. Anytime. I'm ready when you are."

"Let me marry you first," he said, kissing the spot on her neck where her pulse raced. "And then…we start on the honeymoon. For now…let's practice."

He kissed her, and she clung to him. This was it. His forever. It might have taken him years to see it, or even consider it, but it was here. In her arms.

And he was the luckiest bastard in the world.

Acknowledgments

As always, first and foremost I want to thank my husband, Greg. You've always supported me, even when I didn't really want the support and wanted to quit, and you're my number one fan. Here's to many more years and books.

Thanks are due to my children, Kaitlyn, Hunter, Gabriel, and Ameline. Thank you for being so understanding when I say I'm on deadline and need to work. You make some real sacrifices playing those videogames for extra hours when Mom is in a pinch.

To my editors, Candace and Liz, my copyeditor, my managing editor, the blurb writer, the cover artist, the formatter, the publicists, and everyone else who had anything to do with my book at Entangled, thank you for everything you do to make this book shine!

To the rest of my family, thanks for understanding the missed phone calls, parties, and the times I fell off the grid for days and you started to wonder if Greg finally got rid of me. Mom, Dad, Tina, Cynthia, Mom M, Dad M, Erick, Ashley, Connor, Riley, Danny, MeeMaw, and PeePaw—love you!

To my buddies to whom I talked to about this book for endless hours, or whined about deadlines and life in general, you're the real MVP. Jay, Liz, Joanne, Megan, and everyone else out there, I love ya!

Thanks to my agent Louise Fury at the Bent Agency, for your endless work to get me where I want to be. You're the best, and I'm so happy you're my agent. And a special shout out to Team Fury, too!

And last, but certainly not least, a huge grateful thanks to all of you readers out there. It's an honor to write books for you, and for you to enjoy them. See you next time!

About the Author

Diane Alberts is a multi-published, bestselling contemporary romance author with Entangled Publishing. She also writes New York Times, USA Today, and Wall Street Journal bestselling new adult books under the name Jen McLaughlin. She's hit the Top 100 lists on Amazon and Barnes and Noble numerous times with numerous titles. She was mentioned in Forbes alongside E. L. James as one of the breakout independent authors to dominate the bestselling lists. Diane is represented by Louise Fury at The Bent Agency.

CPSIA information can be obtained at www.ICGtesting.com
Printed in the USA
BVOW08s0142281215

431123BV00001B/2/P